Mary Stewart is th[...]
world-famous novels for adults. Her books for
children include *The Little Broomstick* and *A Walk
in Wolf Wood*. *Ludo and the Star Horse* won the
author a Scottish Arts Council Award, and it
received unanimous praise from reviewers on
publication.

Lady Stewart is married to the Emeritus Professor
of Geology of Edinburgh University. She and her
husband have retired from Edinburgh and now live
in the West Highlands of Scotland.

MARY STEWART

Ludo and the Star Horse

Illustrated by Gino D'Achille

Hodder
Children's
Books

A division of Hachette Children's Books

A Catalogue record for this title is available
from the British Library

ISBN-10 0340 93262 7
ISBN-13 978 0340 93262 9

Typeset by Avocet Typeset, Chilton, Aylesbury, Bucks
Printed and bound by Bookmarque Ltd,
Croydon, Surrey

Hodder Children's Books
A division of Hachette Children's Books
338 Euston Road
London NW1 3BH

CONTENTS

For Amélie

CHAPTER ONE

Home

This is the story of something that happened a long time ago, to a boy called Ludo, and you can believe it or not as you please. It was told to me by Ludo's own grandson, and personally I believe every word of it. But you, Amélie, must judge for yourself.

Ludo Spiegl was eleven years old, and he lived in a little mountain village in Bavaria called Oberfeld. Herr Spiegl, Ludo's father, was very poor. He owned three goats and a cow, and that was all, if you don't count his wife and son. Even the old horse he kept for work, and the cottage he lived in, poor as it was, did not belong to him, but to the King, who owned the whole valley and all the land for many miles around.

Herr Spiegl made his living chiefly by carpentry.

He even cut the trees himself, and dragged them down from the mountain with the help of Renti, the old horse, then sawed them up and stacked them and left them to weather. He was a good carpenter, and there wasn't a house in Oberfeld without some of his furniture in it. Even Doctor Kainz, from as far away as Niederfeld, had asked Ludo's father to make him a table; and Herr Spiegl had once carved a seat for the church, which (said the priest) was good enough for one of the King's castles. But the work was slow and hard, and of course it took a long time, so Herr Spiegl had to take any other work that came his way. In summer he and Ludo – whose real name was Ludwig, the same as the King's – left the cottage in the valley and moved up into the mountains with the goats and the cattle from all the valley farms. There the sun shone brilliantly all the time, and there was plenty of good grass and water. This was the Alm, the summer farm. Twice a day all the cows came in from the pastures to be milked, and from this milk Ludo's father and the other men made cheeses, which were stored and later on taken down the mountain and sold. The cheese-making was hard work, in sheds full of steaming vats, and so was the milking. Ludo was too young to help. He spent every day out on the mountain-side watching the cows and goats and seeing that they did not stray. He loved the summer.

But when summer ended life was hard and fierce. Every year, about the middle of September, when dew lay heavy on the grasses, and the butterflies wavered sleepily over the blue scabious and silver thistles, the cattle would trudge, with sweet bells tolling, down the steep mountain paths back to their winter homes in the valley. This was a time of festival in the village, much like our own Harvest Festival; there would be music, and dancing, and the blessing of the cattle, and for a short time life would be full of gaiety and colour; but then the feasting would be over, the cattle would file into their places in the lower rooms of the cottages, and the Spiegls' cow and the goats and Renti would be shut up for the long winter months. Ludo's father would check the store of firewood stacked under the eaves, and would sort out the good seasoned wood for his carpentry, and the household would settle down to the routine of winter.

Then the snow would come.

You have never seen such snow. You would go to bed one night as the flakes began to drift, and the sky was dark, had been dark all day. When you awoke in the morning the sun was out, and what a sun! A blaze in a sky so blue that it hurt the eyes, reflected everywhere from snow dazzling white with clear blue shadows. You could tell where the houses were because the snow was house-shaped. You could see the pine trees because the snow stood glittering in Christmas-tree columns. But that was all. Roads, streams, fields had gone. It was winter, and the snow locked the valleys.

In some ways this was an even better time than summer, because people would get out their snow-shoes and take to the snow. Ludo could never decide which he loved more; lying out in the sunshine at the Alm, watching the goats and cattle peacefully grazing hour by hour; or racing downhill over the crisp and sparkling snow, as swiftly as the King flew by in his golden sleigh with the four grey horses.

But winter could be cruel, too. You could go to bed one evening after a day in the sun and snow, and perhaps if you woke in the night you might hear a small sound like a dog whining at the window's edge. But it wasn't the dog; he was curled beside you in the blankets. It was the north wind; the wicked winter wind that brought the blizzard snow, thick whirling flakes that blotted the world out and drifted deep in the valleys and, worst of all, brought great torrents of snow rushing down the moun-tain-sides. These were the avalanches, which swept away everything in their path and buried it – houses, cattle, people, everything – so deeply that they were never seen again until months later when the snow melted in the spring and the bodies were dragged out to be buried.

It was on one such night that Ludo's story starts.

All the week it had snowed, so that the outlines of village and valley were blurred and soft with snow. Inside the Spiegls' house it was warm and rather stuffy, because nobody with any sense would have opened a window, and indeed Ludo and his father spent most of their day near the big stove in the corner, busy with their winter tasks.

First of all let me tell you what the cottage was like, because, Amélie, it wasn't the kind of house you have ever seen, and probably never will now, though here and there in Bavaria to this day there are tumble-down old wooden huts that look like cattle-sheds, but which were once houses where people like Ludo lived.

The Spiegls' cottage was all made of wood, and was two storeys high. In the bottom storey the animals lived during the winter; they had stalls at one end of the room – we had better call it a barn – while the other end was used as a store-room for the animals' fodder, and also for some of the family's food, like potatoes, and tubs of pickled cabbage which they called sauerkraut, and strings of hard dry sausages, and flour. Then there were Herr Spiegl's tools, and his jars of glue and varnish, and a stack of seasoned wood ready for making into furniture. In one corner stood a box filled to the brim with what looked like the dried roots of trees, and knotty bits of wood broken from dead branches. Which is, in fact, exactly what they were. Besides being good at making tables and chairs, Herr Spiegl enjoyed wood-carving, and almost every evening in winter, when the other work was done and Frau Spiegl sat down by the stove with her sewing, Ludo and his father would sit there, too, whittling away at carvings of gnomes or goats or chamois, which they might be able to sell during the summer to make a little extra money.

It is true that Ludo's carvings did not sell very well – unless his father improved them a bit – because, as his father said to him: 'You will never make a carver until you can talk to the people you carve, and they talk back to you.'

Ludo didn't quite understand what his father meant, because, though Herr Spiegl certainly talked away (to himself, said Ludo's mother, blinking through her spectacles in the light from the stove), Ludo had never heard the little carved gnomes and elves saying a single word. But it must be admitted that, when Herr Spiegl had finished them and hung them on the cottage wall till spring, they looked very lifelike indeed, as if they had affairs of their own and would, as soon as the family was sound asleep for the night, jump down from the wall and go about their own business. And though Ludo's carvings each had two eyes, a nose, and a mouth, all in exactly the right places, they all looked just like pieces of pine-root with no affairs at all.

But still Ludo whittled and whittled, and wished that he could be allowed to help his father with something really useful, like tables and chairs; but he was as clumsy with a plane or a chisel as he could be, and after he had cut himself a few times, and spoiled some good pieces of wood, he was forbidden to do any more. Myself, I think this clumsiness must only have been because he was too eager, and tried to do work which was beyond him, but Herr Spiegl would shake his head impatiently, and wonder aloud what he had done to be saddled with a clumsy son like Ludo, and Frau Spiegl would purse her mouth up over her neat sewing and say that it wasn't everyone who was born with clever hands, but that even Ludo was a bit of a help sometimes; and poor Ludo would hang his head and wish with all his heart that he could do something, even the smallest thing, really well, so that he could be a help to his parents, and perhaps one day hear people in the village saying: 'There goes that clever boy of the Spiegls',' the way they did about Emil the baker's son, and Hans from the smithy, and even Rudi his friend, who had once earned a silver coin for showing the King's huntsman which way the stag had gone. But nobody was ever going to say that about Ludo Spiegl, who had never been to school,

and who did nothing well except carry wood and
fetch water, feed the animals and clean their stalls,
mend the harness, sharpen his father's tools and mix
the glue and clean the brushes and sort the nails and
sweep up the shavings … So he would carve away at
some tough old pine-root (for of course the best
pieces had to be kept for his father) and dream of
one day being a real woodcarver and making things
so beautiful that they were fit for nothing less than
the King's own castle.

Now, the part of his work that Ludo liked best
(apart from the wood-carving, which was really
play) was feeding the animals. Not the cow so much,
because she was rather a stupid creature, or even the
goats, which were clever, but would take advantage
of kindness, and give you a nip or pull loose from
their collars and give endless trouble before they
could be caught again. But he loved the old horse
Renti, whom he had known all his life. Indeed, Renti
was older than Ludo, being now seventeen years old,
which for a working horse is a very good age indeed.
And a working horse he certainly was; he did everything, the ploughing of Herr Spiegl's tiny field, the
dragging of the logs down the mountain-side to be
sawn up, the carting of the cut timber and then the
finished furniture, and a dozen other tasks. For four-
teen years he had done this, and for the last three or
four it could be seen that he was getting slower and

slower; then one day a rolling log caught one of his forelegs and hurt it. By good luck the leg had not broken, but ever since that day Renti had gone stiffly, and a good deal more slowly. So soon, perhaps this next summer, said Herr Spiegl, they would have to get another horse. Neither Ludo's mother or father said a word about what would happen to Renti, but Ludo knew that his father could not afford to feed two horses, so he knew that Renti would be taken away and killed. So every day, when he had finished feeding the other animals, he took Renti his feed and then sat by him, talking to him for company.

'Because I can talk to *you*,' said Ludo, 'and even though I can't hear you, I'm sure you're talking back to me.'

And old Renti would blow gustily into the chopped hay and snuffle with his nostrils at Ludo's chest, and the two of them understood one another very well.

CHAPTER TWO

The Lost Horse

One night, when the wind whined high among the white crags, and the snow swirled thick and ever thicker round the cottage, Ludo sat there, quite alone but for the little gnomes which hung on the walls. His father and mother had gone out, down to the village, because his mother's sister was taken ill, and needed help, and Herr Spiegl would not let his wife journey alone down the valley.

'It will be a bad journey down, he said, 'and a worse journey back. But Ludo will stay here and keep the stove going, and if you have to stay with your sister, why then, I'll come back myself before morning. Because, mark my words, by this time tomorrow there will be no coming and going at all in this valley.'

So Ludo, who was not in the least afraid of the dark or the lonely silence, as you or I might have been, sat there by the stove and carved away at a piece of fir-wood which looked as if it should turn into a very lifelike gnome if you carved a bit here and a bit there.

But it didn't. The wood in the stove hissed and settled, and the wooden clock ticked on the wall, and the eyes of all the gnomes on the log walls watched, just as if any minute they would speak; and below the floor the animals shifted in their stalls and one of the goats whickered, and when the wind fretted too close round the cottage walls the shutters rattled.

Since there was no one to send him to bed, Ludo didn't go. He was cosy near the stove, he had brought in plenty of wood, and he didn't give a thought in the world to economising on the candle. So he sat there carving the gnome's nose and eyes, while the others on the wall watched him, until the door in the clock flew open, and the cuckoo said it was midnight.

It really was time for bed, thought Ludo. And since he slept in the same room, just on the other side of the stove, it wasn't such a hardship to go as it is for us who have to leave a warm room and go up the chilly stairs. He was just putting away his carving tools and the half finished gnome when he was startled by a loud bang, the kind that might be made by a slamming door, or by something heavy falling to the floor. He stood still for a moment, listening. He could hear nothing but the quiet sounds that were the familiar sounds of the night, with behind them all the whining of the wind. Then he realised that the room was colder, as if a door had opened. But the door was fast, and so were the shutters.

So, thought Ludo, the cold draught was coming up through the floorboards. One of the windows in the barn had blown open, and was letting the cold night in.

He picked up the candle, and shielding it with one hand, pulled up the trapdoor in the corner near the door, and climbed down into the barn.

It was bitterly cold down there. In their corner beyond the straw stack the goats were huddled close together for warmth. The cow, stupid creature, just looked at him reproachfully with her big long-lashed eyes. But the horse Renti —

Ludo stood stock-still on the bottom step of the stairs, not believing it. Where the old horse had always stood there was only the frayed end of a rope hanging, still tied to the manger; but no Renti. And the outer door of the barn stood wide open, pushed right back against the piled snow. Renti had gone.

Well, you can imagine that Ludo ran to the open door to peer out in the teeth of the wind, but of course he saw nothing, because the flame was ripped straight from his candle, and outside there was nothing to be seen but the high drifts of snow, and a sort of furrow where perhaps the horse had ploughed his way through them. Already the furrow was no more than a dip in the snow's surface and, though Ludo floundered along it into the dark for a few yards, he couldn't even see the track of it any more. Nor, as far as his good young eyes could strain, did he see any moving thing or any dark shape that could be the truant horse.

Of course it was not really dark, not like a dark, dank night of November here in Scotland, because the snow lay everywhere and reflected back what light there was from the stars. And what stars! In that clear black mountain sky they shone and glittered, and underneath them the snow-peaks glistened, so that someone like Ludo, who was used to the winter darkness, could really see quite well. And while he stood there the wind dropped as suddenly as it had risen, and the snow stopped swirling, except for a few last, silent flakes which drifted down and settled. Everything was still and silent, and very, very cold.

Now Ludo, for all he was clumsy with his father's tools, and not as clever as Hans and Rudi and his other friends in the village, had a lot of common-sense. He knew that the old horse, if he were not recovered and brought back to his warm stable, would die very soon. He also knew that if he himself went out to look for Renti through the deep snow he might fall into a drift himself and not be able to get out of it. In which case he, too, would die.

But it would do no harm to light a lantern and climb the snow-slope behind the cottage, where the view was better. He might catch sight of Renti and be able to follow and bring him home without risk; or, if the old horse saw the lantern, he might struggle back himself out of the cold, and so save his life. If he didn't, all Ludo could do was to go back into the warmth of the cottage, and wait for his father to come back from the village. Between risking his own death and the horse's there could be no choice. He ran in, shutting the barn door behind him, and raced up the stairs to get his thick coat and muffler and his woollen hat with the earflaps. He had thick boots, too, as good as his parents could afford. It did not do to economise on winter clothes in Bavaria. He seized his snowshoes and sticks and ran downstairs where the goats were already munching cheerfully, and the cow paid no attention.

'You don't even care, do you?' said Ludo to them angrily, and pulled the horn lantern down from its hook and lighted it. Then he fastened on his snow-shoes, let himself out of the barn, and closed the door behind him.

He could just see the way up to the alp behind the cottage, because the path lay between two rows of firs, and these made a sort of snow wall to either hand. The snow was very deep, and still soft, so that even in spite of the snowshoes he sank right into it at every step. If you have ever tried to walk through deep snow you will know how hard it was, and this snow was deeper than any we ever have in Scotland. Ludo wanted to hurry, but it wasn't possible to hurry through those soft drifts; so he trudged slowly upwards, stamping each step hard into the snow as he went. He would soon have been exhausted if he had tried to go far, and indeed when he had struggled up to the flat alp above the cottage, he was dripping with sweat inside his clothes, and breathing like a bellows. He stood there, and strained his eyes as far as he could in every direction.

There was no sign of Renti. Nor was there any sign of his father returning from Uncle Franzl's house down in Oberfeld.

Ludo hesitated, wondering what to do. So often, he knew, he did stupid things, and people said: 'It's only Ludo; he's not very bright.' They might say even worse things; they might blame him for Renti's escape. He was the one who mended ropes and harness, so if Renti died (he told himself) it would really be his fault. He knew it was no use going after the old horse, but what he might do, he decided now, was to go down to the village and tell his father what had happened. And if he did, would his father say:

'That was a very sensible thing to do, Ludo,' or would everyone shake their heads at him and mutter: 'There he goes again; bothering his father when his poor Aunt Anna lies so sick.'

So he stood there, and thought about how stupid he was, and how cold the night was, and about Renti with his stiff foreleg, and how by morning the dear old horse would be dead; and he cried, with the tears freezing as they ran down his cheeks.

CHAPTER THREE

The Shooting Star

Possibly it was because of the tears, which filled his
eyes and ran down his face into his muffler, and
made his nose run till he had to wipe it with his wet
glove (and everyone knows how uncomfortable and
miserable that is), besides the unhappiness and the
helpless feeling that he had done something terrible
and now there was nothing he could do about it – but
when the strange thing happened, Ludo didn't notice
it straight away. He just stood there crying for poor
old Renti, out there in the cruel night, and being in a
queer sort of way glad that he could cry his heart out
with no one to see and think he was soft – soppy they
used to call it in my day – to cry like this, especially

17

over an animal. One day he would understand that there is nothing soft about tears when one is bitterly unhappy about something one has done wrong, especially to an animal, which can't defend itself anyway.

So Ludo stood and cried, and all around him stretched the deep unbroken snow of the valley; with the forests above, and above the forests the mountain peaks glittering through the snow-storms that still drifted there like clouds; and above and beyond these still the stars, flashing thick in a black, black sky, and throwing a strange light, like tarnished silver, over the snow wastes. Then far away, at the foot of the great cliff face they call the Jägersalp, something small and black moved slowly against the snow.

It was a marvel that Ludo saw it. He had just wiped his eyes with the nasty wet back of his glove, and he was turning away to go back to the house, when the black moving speck caught his eye. Now, you or I would probably only have seen a black moving speck, but Ludo was used to the great and glittering distances of the mountains, and he had eyes as good as a bird's, which as you know are the best eyes in the world. Also he knew Renti. So he saw straight away that the speck was horse-shaped, and moving like a horse, even though it was forging through breast-deep snow and making very hard going of it.

You would be surprised how those tears dried. His eyes were clear in a flash, and his throat, too. He put both hands to his mouth and gave the long, yodelling call which carries like a bugle-note over the echoing distances of the Alpine country. It was the call he gave in summer to the cows up at the Alm, and it went clear through the night as far as the Jägersalp and came echoing back, moments later, to where Ludo stood.

Renti heard it. He stopped. Even Ludo could not see at that distance just what happened, but he was sure the old horse stopped, lifted his head, and looked back. But then he dropped his head again, leaned his weight against the snow, and forged on, away from home towards the Jägersalp.

And at that instant, two other things happened.

The first was, that the Jägersalp vanished. The steep mountain-side above the cliff began to smoke like a fire. But of course it wasn't a fire. Ludo knew what it was; it was the terrible avalanche, the snow-fall which brings thousands of tons of snow and stones and rock together down like a torrent from the high reaches of the mountains, smothering everything beneath. Somewhere up high above the cliff of the Jägersalp the snow had begun to move, to slip with its own weight; and now a mass of it, gathering and ever gathering, was rushing faster and faster towards the edge of the cliff, and sending up a cloud of snow like white smoke as it moved. It was just above the snowfield where Renti floundered. It had reached the edge of the Jägersalp, and was smoking down over it. And now, soft and sullen, Ludo could hear it, like muffled thunder, tons and tons of snow plummeting down the cliff face and then mushrooming out to bury everything in its path.

There was nothing he could do but stand there and watch. And when the avalanche had stopped and the snow-smoke had cleared away, there was nothing to see but a new, unbroken plain of snow stretching from the foot of the Jägersalp down to the bottom of the valley. Where Renti had been, there was nothing.

Ludo felt as if he himself had been coated in snow and then turned to ice. He couldn't move. He was still standing stock-still, staring at the spot where a moment before Renti had been, when the second thing happened.

A star fell.

From high, high in the winter sky, huge and glittering and beautiful, and looking as if it had been set there by God to shine for ever and ever, the star moved suddenly from its socket and, slowly as a spark drifting from the fire across a dark room, it swam in a long bright curve across the night sky, and all the other stars, still fixed and shining, looked dim beyond it. Behind the moving star, like the tail of a kite, curved a train of sparkling star-dust. Slowly it went, then faster and faster, till suddenly it curved downwards to shoot, like a blazing arrow, right into the plain of snow below the Jägersalp. On the very spot, Ludo could have sworn, where Renti must be.

Then the star's light quenched, and the night was empty as before, and Ludo was alone on the alp above the cottage.

CHAPTER FOUR

The Jägersalp

I don't know what it was about that star, but Ludo then proceeded to forget all the commonsense he had. What he thought he could do I don't know, and I don't think he did either, but something about the sudden, unearthly sight of that star falling from heaven seemed to bedazzle his wits, so that before he even knew what he was doing he had driven his sticks hard into the snow, and was making as fast as he could for the spot where the star had fallen.

He knew the exact spot to make for. If ever you have watched a star fall, you will know how certain you were just where it fell, and if only it were near enough (which it rarely is) you feel you could go straight to the spot and find its cooled, shrunken globe, or the great hole it made where it drove deep into the ground.

I doubt if Ludo really expected to find either of these things; he only knew that the star had fallen to lead him to that spot, and he must go there. So he raced along, and the lights of the village dropped farther and farther behind him till they were out of sight altogether, and there was nothing but the sparkling silence of the night, and the rush of his shoes over the snow.

The shadow of the Jägersalp loomed over him, blacking out the starlight. For the first time he hesitated, and for the first time wondered if he had really done something very foolish indeed. Then all at once the snow gave way abruptly beneath him; a huge crevasse opened directly in front of his feet, and before he could stop himself he had shot clean over the edge and down, down into the dark, soft bottom of the crevasse.

He did not know how far he had fallen, but it seemed a very long way. However, he fell on snow, which was soft, so he didn't hurt himself at all. For a few seconds he lay there, with the breath knocked out of him, then he sat up and, with fingers clumsy from the cold, loosed off his snowshoes. It was pitch dark. None of the starlight could penetrate to the bottom of this black snow-pit. Though he strained his eyes upwards he could not even see where the dark walls of the pit ended and the dark sky began. The crevasse was deep under the shadow of the Jägersalp, and there were no stars to see.

It was very dark, very cold, and very lonely, and Ludo had time now to realise how silly he had been to do what he had done. There was no magic in a shooting star, no message, nothing to send him rushing off into the night like that. In fact he began to remember other things that folk said about stars falling: a falling star, they said, meant a death. So if that lovely star had meant anything at all, it had meant that poor old Renti was dead, smothered under the avalanche. And unless Ludo himself could keep warm and stay alive until his father got home and saw the tracks leading to the Jägersalp, there might be another star falling. For him. Because there was no way out of this pit of snow; he knew that. If he tried to climb and flounder up the sides of it, the new soft snow would cave in and bring with it more and more of the smothering stuff from the slope above, so that even his tracks would be hidden, and his father would have no idea where to start looking.

Ludo sat there, holding his useless snowshoes, and beginning to feel very frightened indeed. The cold grew and grew like ice forming round him, till his eyeballs ached with it, and his body stopped feeling, and he shut his eyes and lay back against a pile of snow as if it were a soft pillow …

Then all at once, right beside him in the dark, the pile of snow began to move. Ludo's eyes opened, he sat up with a start, then jumped aside, his heart thudding. The heap of snow quivered, then it heaved, and then it shook itself, and then it showered down into little heaps on the ground, while what had been inside it got to its feet. Ludo couldn't see anything at all, but he could hear a huffing of nostrils and a shaking of mane and a swishing of tail, and he knew what it was. Old Renti, buried like him at the bottom of the pit, but still alive.

'Oh, Renti!' cried Ludo, and jumped up and flung his arms round the old horse's neck, quite forgetting that when you are at the bottom of a crevasse you have to be very careful indeed not to shout or make sudden movements, for fear of starting another snow-slip.

Which is exactly what happened. With no sound at all, but like a cold gentle fog descending, the sides of the pit caved in, showering down to cover boy, horse, and all.

That is, they covered the place where the horse and the boy had been. But no sooner had the first heralding flakes begun to drift than Renti, with Ludo, you remember, still clinging tightly to his neck and with his face buried in his mane, trotted forward into the blackness, pulling the boy with him. Behind them the snow-pit filled and vanished. Before them, still black, but somehow faintly luminous as if the starlight managed to filter through from above, was a tunnel which led under the snow. Renti broke into a trot almost as if he knew the way, and Ludo, clinging to his mane, ran with him. The tunnel ran straight as a die (if you know what a die is?) for about twenty metres, and as they ran along it, the snow fell in behind them. If they came to the end of the tunnel, Ludo thought, they would come to the end of – well, the end. But there was hardly time to be frightened now, and besides, old Renti did not seem frightened. Indeed, the horse suddenly whinnied, and at the sound, there was a sudden, heavy rush of snow behind them, but in front of them, shimmering in the snowlight, was the solid rock of the Jägersalp, and in it, lighted with a real light, the rich light of torches and candles and leaping fires, an open door.

CHAPTER FIVE

The Cave

The doorway opened on a cave, but such a cave as
Ludo had never seen before. The first impression he
got was of its hugeness, a soaring roof of rock that
vanished into shadow high above his head, and
galleries opening off into darkness in every direction; the second was of the light and warmth. In a
trice the icy coldness had melted from him, his
fingers were warm again and his cheeks glowing,
and when he looked at Renti he saw that the horse's
coat was drying already to its normal chestnut
colour, and that his mane and tail had lost their
bedraggled look and appeared quite thick and

silvery. (Renti was a Haflinger, that tough and hand-some breed of horse with chestnut coats and silver-gilt manes and tails. Some people believe that the sun's own chariot is pulled by Haflingers, and indeed, on a bright day you can well believe it. Ludo did, anyway.)

Then he saw that the cave was full of people. Boys, some of them younger than himself, and some of them looking anything up to sixteen and a little over. They were strangely dressed, in short tunics of skins or wool dyed in dull kinds of colours, and only one or two had shoes, but they didn't look poor – at least, they didn't bear them-selves like poor boys. In fact, the older ones looked arrogant and rather proud, and when they saw Ludo coming shyly across the vast floor of the cave with Renti beside him, three of the older boys got up from their seats round the fire and approached him.

'You're new.' The tallest of them said it rather accusingly.

Ludo didn't quite know what to say to that, so he just touched his forehead as he had been taught to do to his betters, and said nothing.

It seemed to be the right thing to do, for the youth looked a little less stern. He asked abruptly: 'Where did you come from? That way's supposed to be closed.'

'It was the only way I could see,' said Ludo, feeling very puzzled indeed. 'Where is this? I didn't know there was a cave here.'

'How should you?' said the boy, with a lift of his head which made Ludo feel shabbier and poorer than ever. 'We don't make the way obvious to every comer. But you're here, so I suppose you've been accepted, and we shall have to make the best of it. What's your kingdom?'

'Why, Bavaria,' said Ludo, in surprise.

'What? I've never heard of it. Some little outland kingdom, I suppose, with nothing but rocks and a few goats.'

One of the other boys said, from beyond the fire: 'Don't tease him. If the Archer's sent for him, then he's worth something, even if he doesn't look like it. He'll get licked into shape soon enough.'

Ludo didn't much like the sound of this, but at least the second voice was kinder. He said timidly: 'I'm sorry if I came in the wrong way, sir, but —'

'You don't call me sir,' said the first youth impatiently. 'My name is Jason. The Archer's the only one you call sir. You'd better put your horse outside till you need it.'

'If you call that a horse,' said someone from the shadows, and some of the boys snickered. 'What did your father give you that for? Wouldn't the hounds have him?'

Now, Ludo, though he loved Renti and had often said that the old horse understood every word he said, knew that in fact animals don't follow ordinary conversations between human beings. For one thing, they don't find them interesting enough to listen to. But the boy's taunts were near enough to the truth to hurt, and old Renti had been through a hard time and was very tired and looked it, with drooping head and slack ears, so Ludo forgot that he was only a humble peasant's son and these were obviously young noblemen resting after a day's hunting or some such thing, and he flushed right up to his hair and said hotly:

'He's a fine horse, and there isn't any breed better than the Haflingers of Bavaria, and if *you* were as old as he is and had just been buried by an avalanche of snow seven metres deep you'd look a bit sorry for yourself too, I dare say!'

The answer to this wasn't at all what he expected. The tall youth called Jason stared down at him, with his brows drawn together in a sudden frown. 'Snow? You know there has been no snow here yet this winter. What sort of story is that?' And the others all echoed: 'Yes, what sort of story is he trying to tell? Why is he lying? Who is he?' And they got up from their places round the fire and came crowding forward, looking far from friendly. Ludo saw that some of them were armed; they had daggers in their belts and some of them had bows in their hands.

The friendly voice said: 'Steady on, you men, give him a chance.'

Ludo saw now that this was a boy of about four-teen, with a square brown face and strong-looking shoulders. He wore nothing but a kind of kilt made of golden fur splotched with black, which was fastened with a gilded belt that had a long knife stuck through it. As he came forward the other boys made way for him, even the older ones.

He stood squarely in front of Ludo, with his thumbs hooked in his belt. 'Now, suppose you start at the beginning. He usually tells us about any strangers who are due here, but he said nothing about you. You say you are from Bavaria. Well, we've none of us heard of it, but that's nothing to go by: there are a dozen small kingdoms to every stretch of these mountains. – No, wait: you'll get your turn to speak. Now you talk about snow, when we know there hasn't been a fall here since last spring. But I think you were telling the truth, because when you first came into the light there were flakes on your horse's coat.'

He paused. The firelight flickered as loudly as rustling paper. Someone said loudly: 'That's true. I saw it myself,' and someone else said: 'Hush, leave it to Peleus.'

'So,' said the boy called Peleus, 'where does your kingdom lie, and which way did you come?'

'Please, sir,' said Ludo, who had been brought up all his life to be respectful to people who spoke as this boy spoke, however young they were, 'please, sir, it lies out yonder, beyond the Jägersalp, and it stretches farther than I have ever been, and I came in through the doorway there.' And he pointed towards the side of the cave where the snow tunnel had been.

But it was there no longer. The wall of the cave rose behind him in firelit masses of solid rock. There was no sign at all of the doorway through which he had come.

'But it *was* there!' he cried in dismay. 'Renti was caught in the avalanche and I went after him and fell in too, and then we found the tunnel under the snow and saw the door open, and we came in, and ...'

His voice trailed away. The boy Peleus' face had gone as hard as stone, and Jason was reaching slowly for the bow which was leaning against the cave wall. The other boys crowded closer in a half circle, and there was no mistaking their threatening expressions. 'A spy, that's what he is. Who's ever heard of a place called a barbarian name like that?'

'And big, he said, stretching for miles through the mountains – why, we all know there isn't even a valley of that name within seven days' journey from here.'

'Well, but perhaps he came a long way; look at his horse, it's all but foundered.'

'Don't be a fool, he's not one of us; *that* a king's son? And we all know he couldn't have got in through that doorway.'

'But if the Archer sent for him —'

'Look at his face,' said Jason. 'He's never even heard of the Archer. He's an outlander, a paid spy, and it's my vote we ought to treat him as such, and save the Archer the trouble of doing it.'

Ludo had taken a step backwards as they advanced on him, then another. They stood in front of him in a solid wall, unfriendly eyes and grim expressions, and here and there the gleam of a knife. He backed a bit farther, then realised there was nowhere to go, so he stood still. He said desperately, straight to the boy Peleus, who seemed to be some sort of a leader: 'Please, I never said I was a king's son! And I'm not a spy! I'm not! I told you the truth! I went to look for my horse, and we'd both have died if the way into the cave hadn't been open. I don't know who you are or who this Archer is, or what this place is! All I want is to find the way out again and get home!'

His words had the most surprising effect. When he finished there was a sudden and complete silence.

Then he saw that none of the boys was looking at him any more. They had turned and were watching someone who had just come into the firelight from somewhere away in the far shadows of the cave.

CHAPTER SIX

The Archer

'Someone' was the way Ludo first thought of the creature who paced forward into the firelight, but he might just as well have thought of him as 'something'. At first he saw a giant, a tremendously tall man, bearded, with massive shoulders and great muscles across his chest, and fierce dark eyes. He was carrying a great bow, double-curved and fully strung, such a bow as only a giant could string. The firelight glimmered and ran on the gold-tipped horns of the bow, and gleamed on the bare muscles of the giant's mighty chest. He was naked to the waist except for the strap across one shoulder which held the quiver of arrows. Below the waist he seemed to be clothed in hide, or skins, but Ludo couldn't see properly, because the crowd of boys were still in the way. Then they moved aside, and he saw.

The giant was only a giant because where a man's legs would have been, there was the chest and forelegs of a horse. Indeed, the greater part of him was horse, but where the neck and head should have sprung from the shoulders, the man's body reared as high as someone sitting on horseback. You, of course, will know that he was a centaur, but Ludo had never read a book in his life, and had never heard of centaurs. He only knew that here was a being calm and powerful and very dangerous, with all the strength and contradictions of his double nature.

'Who is this?' asked the centaur, and his voice was not human, being full of deep notes and high notes shaken together like a horse's . But what he said was clear.

Ludo merely touched his forehead and said nothing, feeling too much in awe to speak. The boy Peleus answered.

'We were questioning him, Archer. His story is that the doorway was open back yonder in the rock. He comes from some outland barbarian kingdom he calls Bavaria, and he asks us to believe that it is winter there, for the horse fell in a snowdrift, and the boy fell in after it, and found the entrance to this

House under the depths of the snow.'

The Archer stood foursquare over Ludo and Renti, looking down at them with those huge, unhuman eyes. His tail swished against his flanks, which were the colour of mountain sorrel. He said, deep from his chest:

'Is this true, boy?'

Ludo couldn't speak at first. He nodded, swallowed, then managed to croak: 'Yes, sir.'

'You came here by accident? You were not sent by your father the King to be my pupil?'

'My father isn't a king, sir, your worship. The King lives in a castle over in the next valley. I've seen him, sir, my lord, but he would never notice me. My father is Fritz Spiegl, the carpenter, who lives in the cottage halfway up to the Alm.'

'Then how did you come here, and by what charm did you find the gate into my House?'

'My lord, your honour; Renti, that's my horse, sir, broke his tether when the wind blew the barn door open. And he ran away into the snow, with the north wind blowing – that's the bad wind in our country ...' for by now poor Ludo was so confused that he was sure he had somehow travelled many miles from home, not just through a snow tunnel into the Jägersalp; and who is to say he was wrong?

'So, your honour, I knew Renti would die in the snow, so I climbed up the hill till I could see him, and I called him, and he heard me, but he didn't come back. I think that perhaps his wits were astray with the cold. I knew – I thought – that if I went after him I could save him and bring him home. You see, it was my fault about the halter. I'm supposed to mend the harness. If he had died in the snow it would have been my fault. Besides, I – Renti and I – well, sir, I've known him all my life. I had to try and find him …'

All this Ludo told the Archer, not straight through as I have told it, but with many nervous starts and stops, and when he got to the bit about Renti dying in the snow he put an arm round the old horse's neck, not so much out of affection as to support himself, because he really was so nervous that his knees were quaking under him. All the boys stood there, quite silent now, all staring, still with knives and arrows at the ready, and the great centaur gazed down from his height, and it was even less possible to tell what he was thinking than it is to tell what a horse is thinking.

'Then there was the avalanche,' went on Ludo, 'and it buried him, and I – I thought I'd have to go home and leave him out there in the snow. But then the star fell.'

He stopped. The Archer's head had gone up sharply, like a horse tossing its mane. He stood still, but the sorrel hide twitched and glimmered on flank and shoulder with a hint of that unquiet strength.

'A star fell?'

'Yes, sir, please,' said Ludo, holding on tightly to Renti's neck. 'A big star it was, straight out of the sky, and it fell at the foot of the Jägersalp, so I – I followed it, and Renti was there under the snow, and he came this way, and there was a way into the cave, there was really, only it's gone now, and – and —'

Poor Ludo stumbled to a stop. Still nobody moved. There was a long silence, which was broken at length by the Archer. 'Hrrmph,' he said.

Ludo thought that he was just clearing his throat to speak, and looked up nervously, but at the same time Renti raised his head and whinnied, and Ludo realised that the centaur had just spoken to the horse in his own language.

Then for a while the two of them talked. Ludo, of course, couldn't understand a word, nor, it seemed, could the boys, except for Peleus, who looked bright-eyed from one to the other, and his face grew grave and bright by turns. In the end he seemed to be looking at Ludo with pity. But it was a friendly look, and the contempt had gone.

The conversation finished. The Archer blew once through his wide nostrils, like a horse, and then spoke again to Ludo.

'The horse has told me why he left his stable. It was not your fault that he escaped. It was your father who failed to latch the door, and when the horse saw his way free, he bit through the rope himself.'

Ludo opened his mouth to ask why, then shut it again. He thought he could guess. Renti had known that he could not work for much longer, and he had chosen the way out into the snow rather than wait, old and lame, for death. Ludo hung his head in sorrow and shame.

'Yes,' said the Archer gently, 'you have guessed. You must not blame yourself for this, either. It is the way of things. But your horse is one of the race of the star-horses, and he is proud. He chose to go before his time, and return to his own kind. He knew the way into my House, which was the nearest gate into the star country where he must journey. And if you were guided by the shooting star to follow him ... Why, then, we must accept it for a marvel, and allow you entry along with him.'

The boys were looking at one another, surprised, and perhaps a little awed. Ludo, feeling that something was expected of him, said: 'Thank you, your honour,' and waited.

The Archer looked gravely down from his great height. 'So,' he said, 'you are here, and the choice is yours. Will you go with him? It will be a long journey and a hard one. He must follow the path of the greatest star, the one you call the sun, whose chariot travels the high-road through all the Houses of the star country. But for you there is still a way home, back there through the snow. Because you came of your own will, from duty and through love, I will let you go back if you wish. What do you say?'

Ludo took a long breath. At that moment he wanted nothing more than to crawl back into the snow tunnel, and clamber out, if he could, to the surface, and go home. The Archer waited, expressionless. The boys stared. Renti stood with drooping head, and the weight lifted from his lame forefoot.

Ludo looked up at the Archer. 'Can't Renti go back with me?'

'No. There is no choice for him. But there is one for you. Make it now. This horse served you faithfully all his life; now will you serve him, and keep faith with him? If so, I will allow you safe passage through this House. What will happen beyond my borders I cannot tell, nor will it concern me.'

He paused. Somewhere in the crowd one of the boys made a sound of protest, but the Archer ignored it.

'Well, boy?'

'I – I'd better go with him, I think sir,' said Ludo, stammering a little. 'H-he might go astray, or someone might catch him and be cruel to him … Horses don't manage very well on their own, you see. They're a bit stupid sometimes, and they're easily scared, and then they damage themselves and —'

He stopped short. There was a rustle of laughter among the boys. The centaur did not smile, because centaurs never smile, but his tail gave a little double swish, and he shifted his hoofs.

Ludo clapped a hand to his mouth in confusion.

'I – I'm sorry. I didn't mean that. I mean —'

'I know what you mean,' said the Archer. 'You mean to keep faith with your friend. Very well, you shall go with him. You will lead him as best you can along the path the sun is taking, through the good lands and the bad, until you come up with the sun's chariot, or till you reach the end in the House of the Scorpion. The sun left my House this very day. If you can catch him before he reaches this spot again, your life's wish will be granted – or else it will not, and who is to say which of the two will bring more happiness?'

'I don't understand,' said poor Ludo.

'You are not asked to understand. You are asked to do and to endure, to meet joy and danger with what heart you have; you can do nothing else. Go in safety. You have travelled through the House of the Archer without harm, and that is more than may be said of common men.'

He stood aside then, and pointed beyond the firelight, where the cave stretched away into dimness. High on the wall, lit to fierce gold by the firelight, was a great sign like an arrow: ⫩

Under this a tunnel led out of the cave. Ludo, who had been too awed to take in much of the rather grand speech of the centaur's, hung back, thinking of a hundred more questions he would have liked to ask, but Renti limped forward without hesitation, bowing his head to the Archer as he passed. So Ludo just said: 'Thank you, sir,' very humbly, and followed the horse.

Before he had gone three steps one of the boys said earnestly: 'Sir, if he is going on a quest, and such a quest, should he not have with him a charm, or a spell, such as a ring or a goblet —'

'Or a shield that turns enemies to stone,' said another.

'Or a ball of twine that will lead him by the right path,' cried a third.

The Archer shook his head. He gave that little double swish of the tail again, and his voice was more human than before.

'Enough of charms and magic. It is his own nature which will bring him home, even as it brought him here. To be clever is one thing, to be true and brave is another, and if a peasant's son has that, why, he has less need of charms and weapons than a king.'

All the same, just as Ludo and Renti got beyond the range of the fire's glow there came the swift rush of light feet behind them, and the boy Peleus caught them up. Ludo felt the cool hilt of a long knife slipped into his hand, and a whisper in his ear:

'Here, take it, you may need it. What he says is all very fine, but I've been around and I know. Good luck, and we'll look for you, a year from today.'

Then he was gone, and boy and horse were alone in the long rock passage, plodding towards the light at the far end.

CHAPTER SEVEN

The Goat

To Ludo's surprise it was quite light outside. In fact, a whole day seemed to have passed, because the sky was rosy, as if drawing towards sunset. The sun itself was not visible, but its rays shone strongly out from behind one of the mountain peaks to Ludo's right.

He stood at the mouth of the cave with his hand on Renti's neck. The boy Peleus had run back into the cave and disappeared. The two of them, boy and horse, were alone among the mountains.

It seemed as if they had come out on the other side of the Jägersalp, into a valley that Ludo had never seen before. But it was strange in more ways than

45

one; there was no snow, only slopes and screes and towers of shining white rock that flushed to apricot in the rays of the vanishing sun. Below the flat stretch of rock where they stood was a lake of cloud which hid all the lower countryside from them. Though the air was chilly at this height, it was not cold, and when Ludo put a hand down to touch the rock beside him, he found in it a lingering warmth from the day.

'Well,' he said aloud to Renti, 'the sun has been out today after all. I suppose we had better do as he said, and follow it.'

Indeed, there seemed to be no choice. The only way from the cave mouth was a broad, rough track which led to the right, and climbed round a jutting crag.

Ludo took hold of Renti's halter, not so much to lead the horse as to help him over the rough going. 'Come on, then,' he said, and the two of them started to climb the track, their shadows long behind them in the rosy light.

The track grew steep and yet steeper, and narrower, too. The rocks were loose, and sometimes rolled alarmingly under their feet. Ludo was used to mountains, and could climb like one of his own goats, but old Renti had not been to the high alps for a few years, and besides, he was going very lame. Ludo was worried about him, and went slowly; more slowly than he liked, for the light was fading, and the air grew colder. Also, he was hungry, and he knew that Renti must be hungry, too. And there was nothing for either of them. There was nothing but rock, no living thing. No bird, no bush, not so much as one of the dry alpine thistles that grew even at this height in his own valley.

'If we could even see a goat, we'd know there must be something for you to eat,' said Ludo. He himself could go without, but poor old Renti wouldn't understand.

And just as the thought came into his mind, he did see a goat. It was just a shadow, staring down from above him, with the last of the sun glinting on its yellow eyes. Then it moved, and Ludo could see that it was not one of the wild mountain goats, but a big black goat very like the leader of the flock that he minded in the summer. And where there was a flock, there would surely be a goat-herd. Ludo put his hands to his mouth and sent another of those yodels echoing up into the rocks.

'Don't make such a noise,' said someone crossly. 'You'll wake all the others up.'

Ludo stopped dead in his tracks and looked all around him. But he could see nobody; no living thing except Renti and the goat. And of course Renti couldn't talk, not to him. But the goat — ? He saw that Renti was looking at it, head up and ears pricked intently.

The goat now came down from its high eyrie. It came casually, carelessly almost, stepping lightly from one invisible foothold to another until it landed, with a click of its four neat black hoofs, on the track in front of Ludo and the horse. It put its black head on one side and regarded him with clever, cold eyes.

'So you got this far,' it said. 'I wouldn't have thought you could. The Archer doesn't let many through. It must be because of the horse. He's got a weak spot for them, which is only natural when you come to think about it ... It can't be for your sake. You're only a little boy, and not very bright at that, and he only accepts —'

'Is it really you talking?' asked Ludo. Perhaps the goat was right about his not being very bright, but he can hardly be blamed for being a bit slow in the uptake. The setting sun was streaming down between a gap in the peaks, and the shadows were blue and long and dark, and the goat, which was almost twice the size of the ones in his flock at home, was coal black with long hair which shone like spun jet, and shimmered in the sunset light reflected from the rocks. Its eyes were wise and cold and golden, and thoroughly untrustworthy.

'Not very bright,' repeated the goat. 'Of course it's me talking. Who else? Not that wretched beast you've got in tow, for all he's seen better days.'

'He's a star-horse!' said Ludo, stung.

The goat laughed. If you know goats as well as Ludo did, you'll know that even common goats can laugh, and often do, always at human folly. Then it nodded, and the magnificent horns glimmered as if they had been polished. 'So that's it, is it? You're following the sun. Well, you won't get far, but I've nothing against you, so I'll put nothing in your way. In fact, I might even help you.' He snuffed consideringly, lowering his chin into his silky beard, and slanting a long look up at Ludo. 'I've heard of you, my boy, and though you're simple, you've been good to some of my people, and they speak well of you.'

At that moment a sound came from above, where the goat had first appeared. A sound completely familiar to Ludo; the pattering and tapping of small tidy hoofs on rock; a herd of goats. They came streaming over the summit of the crag, and skipped down the same way as the black goat, neat and dainty and unhesitating, a hundred or more, coming down the crag like a white and grey and tawny waterfall, with tossing horns and yellow eyes. But these were ordinary-sized goats, and none of them spoke. They crowded round Ludo and Renti and the black goat, bleating with curiosity.

'Why,' said Ludo suddenly, making a discovery, 'there's Heidi, and Lotti, and little Sisi!' He turned on the black goat, which was watching him with a glint of amusement in those golden eyes. 'They're from my flock! They fell into a gully last spring when the rock came down after the storm, and I thought they were dead!'

The black goat shook his horns.

'Yes,' he said, 'and you climbed down three times to find them, and you never left the place till you were sure there was no hope for them. I told you I'd had reports.'

Ludo was bending over his own three goats, which crowded close for him to rub the base of their horns. 'Lotti looks marvellous! I think she looks better than ever she did! And Heidi —' He broke off. He had just noticed something about Heidi. She had been an old goat, with a jagged scar across her face, and hoofs slightly overgrown. But now she had none of these things. Her face was whole and sleek, and her hoofs were neat as a kid's. Yet it was unmistakably Heidi, with the tawny blotch over her right eye – and besides, she was rubbing her head against Ludo just as she always did. And then the third goat … Ludo remembered now, vividly, his last sight of little Sisi lying on the ledge half-way down the cliff, with what was obviously a broken neck, and blood all over her coat. Now she skipped up to him and reared prettily for him to pull her ears.

Ludo looked over their heads at the black goat, who nodded. 'Yes, I see you've guessed. They were dead. I told you there was nothing more you could do for them. I did it all.'

'So I can't – I can't take them back with me?'

'No. Nor will they want to go. You will leave them here with me.'

Ludo swallowed hard. 'And who are you – sir?' If anyone had told him that he would ever call a goat 'sir' he would have thought they were mad. But then if anyone had told him he would ever stand on a mountain pass talking to a goat, he would have thought the same thing.

'You may call me Goat,' said the black goat.

Poor Ludo found that he was shivering. He tried three times before he managed to ask the next question, which you, I imagine, will have been asking yourself for some time already.

He asked, in a whisper, for he was really very frightened: 'Am I dead, too?'

The goat snickered. It was a heartless sound, but rather reassuring. 'You soon will be,' he said, 'if you stand here wasting time till the sun goes down. You've got to get over the pass before dark, my lad, for if you're there when night comes you'll die of the cold. Go on, I'll not stop you. You don't need me to show you the way; you can't miss it. It'll take you across the watershed and down as far as the spring. After that you'll have to look after yourself.'

As he finished speaking he turned and leaped, all four feet together, on a goat-path as narrow as a ribbon, right above the track where Ludo stood. The sun's last light flared on the shining horns, and the yellow eyes looked suddenly, thought Ludo, mocking and wicked.

He called out desperately: 'Goat! Sir Goat! Please don't go yet! Where does the path go to? Please tell me where this is, and whose country it is?'

'It's my country,' said Goat, 'and I said I wouldn't harm you. What more do you want? And I told you where the path went ... Do as I say! Climb, always climb! There's nothing else to do, is there? There is power in height and strength in rock and glory in space! Always climb! As long as you can move, go upwards, till you can look down, down on every-thing ... Go to the top of the world. That is where I live.' And his eyes were cold and hard as the rock itself. 'Good-bye,' said Goat, giving Ludo one last look with the light striking back off the yellow eyes, then he turned and, with one great leap, vanished over the top of the crag. The other goats, like metal filings drawn by a magnet, streamed after him. Up the cliff face, over the crest of the now invisible ridge, went the tapping and pattering and the rustle of falling dust, then the sounds died away in the silence.

Ludo ran to the bottom of the cliff and stared upwards after the flock. Nothing. Nothing but the empty rocks and the dark shadows deepening to black. The sun had gone, and the air was suddenly much colder. He shivered, and stroked Renti's neck. The old horse had followed him, limping, and now stood with lowered head and drooping ears, looking tired and dispirited.

'It's all right,' said Ludo, trying to sound as if he meant it. He was trying to make himself believe that he was dreaming, and that at any moment now he would waken up by the stove at home, with Renti safe and warm in the barn below, to find that the whole adventure had been a bad dream.

But he did not wake, not even when an icy little current of wind raised goose-pimples on his neck, and stirred Renti's mane. Ludo swallowed the lump in his throat, took a firm hold on the horse's halter, and said briskly and rather loudly:

'Come on. He said we had to get across the top before dark, and it's almost dark already. There's nothing for it but to try. Hold up, Renti, we'll manage.'

And they did. The boy was exhausted and the horse was limping very badly indeed by the time they mounted the last steep climb to the top. But suddenly it really *was* the top, and after zigzagging to and fro between steep screes half covered with snow, and crags which soared straight up into the dark like towers, the track suddenly slanted downhill.

It was deep dusk now, and Ludo wondered if they dared stop yet; but after a while he remembered something else Goat had said: 'Go as far as the spring' … They would surely hear a spring? And Goat had implied – if he was to be trusted – that they would be safe if they got that far. At any rate they could have a drink, and creep somewhere in among the rocks till daylight. Ludo hugged one hand to his empty stomach and led Renti, slipping and stumbling with weariness, down the loose shale of the track till, as suddenly as a bird's song in the black empty air, they heard the trickle of water, and knew they must have reached the spring.

CHAPTER EIGHT

The Water-Carrier

The sound of the water came from some way to one side of the track. Ludo hesitated, hardly daring to turn off into the rocky wilderness. In the deep darkness it was impossible to see, and only too easy to take a false step and perhaps plunge over the edge of the steep rock and fall into space.

But Goat had been clear enough about finding the spring, and besides, Ludo was fiercely thirsty. The thought of water was tempting, and worth a risk. What was more, they couldn't go on in the darkness; they would have to wait somewhere till the stars came out and gave them light.

Renti thought so, too. As Ludo hesitated the old horse, head stretched eagerly forward, pushed past him and began to thread his stumbling way between the boulders towards the water. Ludo ran after him and took hold of the halter again. They felt their way forward together. If only, Ludo was thinking, the water is easy for poor Renti to reach. I can climb to it, but he can't, and I've nothing to carry it in …

The sound of the spring grew louder. They quickened their pace. All of a sudden they came round a corner of the cliff, to find themselves at the edge of a wide flat space, like a small field, which lay in the shelter of the encircling cliffs. The spring was there, a trickle of water gushing from a crack in the cliff and falling into a round pool from which a little stream overflowed and ran downhill. On the rim of the pool stood a big stone jar.

And to Ludo's surprise, they could see it all quite clearly. Beside the pool was a hut, and from the open door of the hut came the most lovely warming glow of firelight and lamplight. And with the light came the smell of hot sausages, and the sizzling sound of frying.

Now, not only was Ludo very hungry indeed, but sausages were his most favourite food of all. He was also tired and still rather frightened, but he dropped the halter, and almost ran forward towards the hut. Renti, who was not concerned with sausages, pushed past him to the water and lowered his head to drink. Ludo ran to the doorway of the hut and looked inside.

The hut was small, with wooden walls and a thatched roof; planks made a rough flooring, and between the planks were gaps through which the draughts crept. But at the far side was a fireplace, where logs burned merrily, and beside this stood a low table made out of thick, roughly planed wood, and a stool, such as Ludo's father made. On the table were two wooden platters and a jar and two tumblers. There was a rug made of skins lying before the fire, and on this knelt a boy, frying sausages in a huge frying-pan.

The boy didn't seem to have heard anything, though Renti's hoofs had made plenty of noise on the rock. Ludo stood shyly in the doorway, but the smell of the sausages was making his mouth water and even giving him a griping hunger pain in his stomach, so he nerved himself to rap at the open door and clear his throat and say, 'Please. Excuse me. Please may I come in?'

The boy said, without turning: 'Supper's ready. You've taken your time, haven't you? I began to think you'd gone straight past.'

Ludo advanced towards the fire, slowly at first, then, as the boy didn't move but just went on turning the sausages in the pan, he got to the fireside with a rush, and held his hands out to the blaze. It was wonderful. If you have ever stayed out too late, past bedtime, without supper, and if you've been tired and a bit unhappy as well, you'll know how it felt to Ludo to get inside that crude little hut with the hot blazing fire and the smell of food.

'Go on,' said the boy, 'sit down. How many can you eat?'

The only time anyone ever asked Ludo a question like that was on his birthday, which was on June the first, and even then only if Herr Spiegl had managed to make a good sale during the month before. And the boy really seemed to want to know. He lifted the pan from the fire, and now Ludo could see that it was full of the most glorious sausages, big and brown and crisp and sizzling; and here and there, where the boy had pricked them with a fork, the rich meat was oozing and crinkling out of them. To one side of the pan were slices of fried potatoes, and some fried onions smelling glorious, browning nicely in the smoking fat. There must be at least twenty sausages.

Ludo swallowed. His mouth was really watering quite embarrassingly. 'Four, please,' he said, because he was a polite little boy.

'Hold the plate, then. Do you want fried potatoes too?'

'Yes, please.' Ludo held one of the wooden platters, and the boy put six sausages on it (then why did he bother to ask me? thought Ludo happily) and a gorgeous mound of potatoes and fried onions. 'Help yourself to bread and butter,' said the boy, and began to pile his own platter. 'Well? Why don't you sit down?'

'There's only one stool,' said Ludo. Now that he was feeling warm he had time to look around him, and when the boy turned Ludo could see that he was not just a goat-herd or a shepherd boy. He was dressed very much like Ludo, in warm-looking trousers and a tunic worn thigh-length over them, but Ludo's clothes were poor and patched, while this boy's were made of good stuff in bright, lovely shades of deep blue and peacock blue, and his belt was studded with what Ludo took to be glass beads, but nobody ever saw glass that flashed so brilliantly, and with so many colours. You and I might guess that they were diamonds, and know that the boy was someone very important indeed, but Ludo had never seen a diamond in his life. Still, he waited till the boy gestured once more, impatiently, towards the stool, and then he sat down, while the boy curled on the rug and started to eat. Thankfully, at last, Ludo fell on those sausages and onions and fried potatoes and big warm chunks of bread from the brand-new loaf …

I can't tell you exactly how many sausages there had been in that pan, but when the boys had finished there were none at all, and I believe Ludo ate most of them. When at last he put the platter down with a satisfied sigh, and drank a tumblerful of water to follow the sausages, he felt marvellously different, not a bit tired, and not at all sleepy.

'Thank you very much,' he said. 'That was wonderful, and this water – why, it's the best I ever tasted. What spring is that outside?'

'The water doesn't come from the spring,' said the boy. 'It comes straight from the sky.'

'Rain-water?' Ludo drank this at home, from the barrel, but it never tasted a quarter as good as the spring water he carried for his mother. 'It's different from ours,' he said, and grinned when the boy laughed. 'Well, I know it's the same, but it tastes different.'

'That's because you needed it so badly. And the food, too.'

'Well,' said Ludo – he felt quite at ease with this boy, though he had been frightened of the ones in the cave – 'I must say I've never had sausages as good as those in my life. I expect they saved my life, as a matter of fact. I thought I was going to have to sleep out on the mountain without food or water. I know there'd have been snow to eat, but that never tastes right, somehow.'

'The snow won't lie,' said the boy. 'It never does lie here, the rain washes it away.'

'Rain? We never get rain at this time of year,' said Ludo.

'Haven't you ever heard of February Fill-the-Ditch?'

'But it's not February —' began Ludo, then stopped, because he remembered how queer everything had been, and how the boy Peleus had said, 'See you next year.'

'It's always February,' said the boy. He was sitting cross-legged on the rug, staring at Ludo. He had wide cheekbones and a wide mouth and eyes which slanted up at the corners and were long and narrow and the most vivid blue. His hair was black, and very untidy.

Ludo didn't understand, but there was so much that he didn't understand that it seemed hardly worth saying so. He said instead: 'I'll do the washing-up for you,' and picked up the platters.

The boy shook his head. 'Just put them outside. They'll be clean in a moment.'

Ludo was puzzled, but he did as he was bidden. As he stooped to lay the platters and the frying-pan on the ground near the door he saw that the stars were out now, giving quite a strong light, and near the hut old Renti was grazing on a patch of thick, good grass. As he stood there he felt a heavy drop of rain, then another, and as he scurried back indoors to the firelight he heard the rain start in earnest. Renti, of course, took no notice; he was used to grazing in rain or shine; and the air was warmer than it had been on the other side of the pass.

'Now,' said the boy, 'you had better tell me your

name and what you are doing on that road.'

'My name's Ludo, short for Ludwig Spiegl, and I'm trying to find the way back to the other side of the Jägersalp.'

'You've a long way to go, then.'

'But surely it's only just on the other side of the pass? I came through a cave in the bottom of the cliff —'

'You came through the Archer's House, and then through the Goat's. You're a long way from home already,' said the boy, but he said it kindly. 'You'll have to go all the way now. Didn't the Archer explain?'

'Nobody explained,' said Ludo, 'not really.'

'I don't suppose they would. The Archer's too toplofty, and the Goat goes his own way and cares for nobody. But at least you got this far. That says quite a lot for you. I'll help you myself, that goes without saying. But you'll come across those who won't.'

'Who are you?' asked Ludo.

'You can call me Gula. I own the country down as far as the cataract. I'll help you that far, but I can't guarantee what will happen after that.'

He was silent for a while, the long brilliant eyes narrow and thoughtful, dwelling on Ludo, but looking as if they saw right through him. Ludo sat silent too, not liking to speak. He knew now that this boy must be a prince, but he felt too safe and too full of food to be frightened. They sat there listening to the crackle of the fire, and the drumming of the rain on the thatch.

'Now,' said Gula, 'you can tell me your story, right from the start.'

So once again Ludo told his story, from the moment when he heard the barn door slam. The boy listened without stirring, watching with those narrow, vivid eyes.

When Ludo finished, he nodded. 'Yes, I see. I couldn't understand why the Archer had let you through. He doesn't usually. That gang of his are always spoiling to show how good their training has been ... But he'd do it for the horse; if the horse wants to make the journey, then the Archer will let you go with him. The horse probably asked him to. Did he?'

'I don't know. They talked together, but of course I didn't understand. He just said to me that I could go with the horse or not, as I chose. So I said I would. It seemed to please him. He told me we would have to follow the sun, and catch him before we got to the – I think he said the Scorpion. One of the boys – he was kind, actually – said "See you a year from today". That was all.'

'Well,' said Gula, 'it will take you a year. If you get round, that is.'

'A year?' cried Ludo in dismay. 'But I must be home long before that to look after the goats and cattle! They'll be let out in May, and later my father goes up to the Alm —'

'Don't worry,' said Gula kindly, 'it won't seem like a year. They won't even know you've been out of the valley. If, that is, you get back at all.'

'You said something like that before. Do you mean – do you mean I might meet other people, like those boys, who might want to kill me?'

'I'm afraid so. But it's a risk you'll just have to run. You can't go back now, even if you changed your mind and left your horse to find his own way. You'll have to go on. But you ought to be able to get through some of the Houses without being seen at all, and the others – well, you'll maybe talk your way through them, if you find fighting doesn't help. Talk first and fight afterwards is a very good motto.'

'Fight? But I can't fight.'

'Why not? You're a strong boy, and you're armed.'

'Oh.' Ludo had forgotten the knife that Peleus had given him. It was stuck through his belt, and looked very long and sharp and rather deadly in the firelight. Somehow the sight of it was no comfort at all. 'And as for talking, I never was much good at that. They're always telling me at home,' said Ludo, and at the thought of home he felt a very unboylike lump in his throat, 'that I'm stupid.'

'What does that matter? There are better things than being clever,' said the boy Gula.

It was so nearly what the Archer had said that this time Ludo was impressed. 'What things?'

'"Deal faithfully, live cleanly, breathe sweet breath",' said the boy. He said it in a special voice, the sort of voice that Ludo's mother used when she was reading aloud, or the priest used when he was talking in church on a Sunday. But it did not come at all strangely from this blue-eyed boy squatting cross-legged in a herd's hut in the mountains. Outside, the rain had stopped. The sound of Gula's voice echoed from somewhere in the high starry rocks, and re-echoed farther away, as if in the stars themselves, and then died. There was no sound but the tearing of the good grass as Renti grazed, and the dot-and-carry-one tread of his lame hoofs.

Then Gula grinned and said, in a boy's voice again: 'You can bring the dishes in now, and I'll tell you what it's all about before we sleep. I'll have a lot to do in the morning.'

Ludo obeyed him, while Gula put more logs on the fire, and then handed him a thick, gay blanket in a diamond pattern of sapphire and dark blue. Gula wrapped himself in another with a marvellous design of peacock's eyes, and they both settled down, one to either side of the fire.

'Now,' said Gula, 'listen hard, because I can only tell you a little, and after you leave here, which you'll have to do in the morning, I can't help you at all …

You said you came from Bavaria?'

'Yes.'

'I have seen it,' said the boy, thoughtfully, with that faraway and dreaming look again. Ludo thought it was a strange way of putting it, but he said nothing. 'I have seen the King in that swan-boat of his, on the waters in the moonlight … I am not sure yet, but I think that he will come through my House …' The beautiful brilliant eyes fastened on Ludo again. 'But you will not come again. Now listen. You are going with the old horse to catch the sun. This means that you must go fast and far, and you will probably never catch him, because you are on foot and your horse is old and lame, whereas the sun drives a chariot with four horses, the finest that were ever seen in your world and out of it. But if you follow the sun's track, and have courage and a bit of luck, you may succeed.'

Ludo swallowed, and nodded, and said nothing. There was nothing to say.

'Now, on his way through the sky, the sun must drive his chariot through twelve kingdoms, each one with its ruler, and each one with its own fixed stars and straying stars and its own ways and its own laws. The sun is the only being who by law may pass through them all. If you follow him, you are beyond the law. Men may pass through some, but only a few have ever made the whole circuit. In fact,' said Gula, sounding all at once just like a boy again, 'I don't think much of your chances. But I think it's a pretty good try, and if you do succeed, why, life will never be quite the same again in your valley.'

Ludo thought this would be a pity, but was too polite to say so. It was also not much use regretting what had happened. He might not be bright, but he knew that once you have started something, it is silly not to finish it. Besides, he had to; there was no going back.

'So this is your kingdom?' he asked.

'I call it my House. Yes. You've nine more to go, and if you go well and fast you will catch the sun before he gets round to the Archer again. All you have to do is follow the track – you can't miss it, believe me – and dodge trouble as best you can. There's no advice I can give you about that, because most of the rulers are pretty unpredictable. How they treat you depends on a lot of different things. They'll feast one man – as I've feasted you – and kill the next as soon as look at him. You can't ever tell till it's happened, and then it's too late. But —' he leaned forward and his voice went grave and grown-up once more – 'there are one or two who are always dangerous, and these you must shun. Don't try to fight or to reason. Just hide and run until you are across their borders.'

'Y-yes?' said Ludo. He was wondering how one

hid a full-sized horse who was too lame to run, but Gula seemed to have forgotten this problem.

'The Twins,' said Gula. 'They're a couple of thugs, kill you before breakfast, just to get up an appetite; and the Wolf-lord who hunts with them is worse. He's the Archer's brother.'

'Is he a man-horse, too?'

'A centaur? No, he's – I can't describe him exactly, but you'll know him when you see him. They call him the Far-Shooter. If he so much as sees you, you're doomed. The only way to escape him is to go through that House by night. He can't see by moonlight. But the one after him is worse still. That's the Crab. This is where the difficulty lies, because the Crab sees best by moonlight. If you run too far, and blunder across his border, he'll get you; and believe me, he'll crunch you and your horse up, snip-snap, before you even get half across the sand.'

'But how do I know —' cried Ludo, who had been wondering this for some time – 'how do I know where the borders are? There was nothing to show on the way here – no frontiers, no wall, not even a river or a bridge.'

'There were signs, but you didn't know what to look for. See, here they are.' He handed a paper to Ludo. 'Keep that, and don't lose it. It'll show you what to look for.'

'I – I can't read,' said Ludo, ashamed.

'You don't need to. I told you they were signs. No, the other way up.'

Ludo looked at the paper in the firelight. It held twelve signs, set in an arc like a rainbow's arc, and looked like this:

The boy's finger rested on the one marked: ♒

'This is where you are. And the next House is the House of the Fish. I think you'll manage that one, coming from me. After them, the Ram and the Bull – they're anybody's guess. Then, if you get through, it's the Badlands next, of the Twins and the Crab. I can't tell you any more, but there they all are, right round to the Archer again. You have to finish before that, of course. There. See?'

He was pointing to the sign before the Archer's. It was: ♏

'What is that?' asked Ludo, though he was beginning to think he had very little hope of getting that far.

'The Scorpion,' said Gula, shortly.

'What's he like?'

'He is the last.'

'Yes, I know, but —'

'He is the last,' repeated Gula, and would say no more. 'Now, I've told you all I can. Put that paper safely away and go to sleep. I've a lot of work to do tomorrow.'

'Work? You? What sort?'

'Fetching water from the spring.'

'I'll do it for you. I do it for my mother.'

'You couldn't do it for me,' said the boy, and laughed. 'That's my job. I'm February Fill-the-Ditch himself. They call me the Water-Carrier. Go to sleep.'

CHAPTER NINE

The Fish

When Ludo awoke in the morning it was raining again. The door of the hut was open, and through it came a grey, sodden light and that smell of snow melting which is the wettest smell in the world. The fire was out, and the boy was gone.

Ludo would have thought that last night had been a dream, except for the sight of the two wooden platters and the mugs, and the clean frying-pan hanging where Gula had put it. He rubbed the sleep out of his eyes and unrolled himself from his blanket and ran to the door and looked out.

Rain, slanting heavily from a low sky, and striking

the rock with splashes like a fountain turned full on. Old Renti, huddled close under the wide eaves, in the only patch of shelter there was. Lumps of dirty snow, newly brought down from the rocks above the pass, being hammered to wetness and washed away while he looked at them. But still no Gula.

Then he noticed that the big jar had gone from the edge of the pool. So Gula had really meant it when he said he was going to carry water today! As if there were any need … !

Although Ludo was hungry again, he did not quite like to start eating without his host; but as he looked longingly at the table he noticed a piece of paper beside the loaf, skewered to the table-top by a knife.

He went reluctantly to look at it – reluctantly, because he could not read, and was afraid that the message might be important. Which it certainly was – but he could understand it perfectly, because on the paper there was nothing but a big arrow drawn, which pointed to the remains of the loaf and a big jar of honey which stood beside it. So Ludo had breakfast, and took the liberty of breaking off an extra bit of the loaf – which was very big – to put in his pouch for later, then he washed his mug and platter again, and said 'Thank you' aloud to the absent Water-Carrier, and went out into the rain.

And what rain! I doubt if you have ever seen rain like it, and I'm certain that you never want to. It was as thick as stair-rods, and poured down like a blinding bead curtain in front of Ludo and Renti as they picked their way down the track, so that they could hardly see where to put their feet. Worse still, it came down so hard that it tore great chunks of the track clear away from under them, or brought lumps of rock and streams of mud and gravel thumping down from the high rocks to either side of them, so that in places the track was almost knee deep in a sliding slab of mud, and in others was pitted like a honeycomb with deep holes full of water, where you could break an ankle if you stepped in without looking. And once, just as they had slipped and slithered down through one especially bad bit, the whole track, with a roaring noise even louder than the roar of the rain, suddenly slid sideways from behind them and vanished over the edge of the precipice below. This frightened them both so much that they began to hurry, which wasn't a wise thing to do, and was certainly not easy. They were so occupied with keeping their feet in the treacherous deluge of mud and water that when they passed a boulder bearing a sign on it that was on Gula's paper, Ludo didn't notice it. ✕

Without even knowing it, he and Renti had stumbled and slithered into the House of the Fish.

* * *

They were a long way down the track by this time, and almost off the mountain. But the rain was too thick to see what lay ahead, though now Ludo knew that it could not be his home valley. In fact, by the time he and Renti had gone three or four miles farther he didn't really care where they got to, as long as they got out of the rain. At length they found themselves splodging – wading sometimes, even – along more level ground, where all the countless streams from the mountains, swollen by the rain, had joined together into a big river which roared along, tossing foam the colour of fish-scales as high as their heads, and sometimes, suddenly, whirling frighteningly right across their path, as if it was stretching out a wet grey arm to grab them.

Then, all at once, they came to the end of the track.

At first Ludo couldn't believe it. He stopped, with the water swirling and sucking round him, now soaking his already sodden feet, now flooding right up to his knees, the strong current tugging as if it meant to drag him away with it. And indeed, it looked as if this was exactly what would happen. The river had spread out ahead of them, and the track was flooded completely. Where it had been there was a wide gorge walled by high cliffs, completely filled with moving water.

'But Gula said the track went the whole way!' cried Ludo in dismay. 'How can we follow it? It's right under water!'

Renti didn't reply. He looked terribly dejected, soaking wet, with his rough chestnut coat plastered down with mud, and his mane and tail, which should have been rather a pretty silver-gilt colour, dark with mud and all stuck into rat's tails.

Ludo patted the horse's soaking neck, then reached into his pouch for the bread.

'Let's have a snack while we think what to do. Here's your half.'

In fact he gave the horse a good bit more than half, which seemed to him only fair, since Renti's stomach was a great deal bigger than his own. The bread was, of course, sopping wet, but Renti munched his and looked a bit perkier, and Ludo himself felt better.

'Renti,' he said, stroking the old horse's nose, 'you do want to find the sun, don't you? Because we can't go back; they all say so. So even though we can't see it, the track must be there, under the flood.' He added, rather more loudly, for he needed to reassure himself as much as Renti: 'Gula said we had to go fast, so I don't think we dare wait for the flood to go down. I think we have to go on, even if it means wading …'

His voice faltered. The water did look very deep, and it was running very fast, piling through the gorge between the cliffs. Ludo swallowed. 'Do you think,' he said to Renti, 'that it would hurt your foot too much if I sat on your back, just for a short while? If I don't, I'm going to be out of my depth very soon, and I can't swim.'

You would have thought that Renti had understood every word, which may of course be true. He made the little whickering sound he had made to the Archer, and tossed his dripping head up and down as if he was nodding, so Ludo clambered up on to the wet back, and, with the boy clinging tightly to his long mane, the old horse forged carefully forward into the flood.

For about a hundred metres they managed beautifully. They must still have been on the track which, though invisible under the grey-green flood, was fairly level. But then Ludo became conscious of two things; first, that the water was still rising; and second, that they were being jostled by something underneath it, and that at any moment Renti might lose his footing and plunge them both into the torrent.

Which is exactly what happened. At one moment they were ploughing slowly ahead, with the horse's head held up well above the surface, and the angry river washing over Ludo's thighs, then suddenly something seized Ludo by the leg and dragged him clear off the horse's back. At the same moment Renti lost his footing and plunged headlong into the flood.

The next few moments seemed a lifetime long. Ludo was holding tightly to the horse's mane when he fell, and instinctively he still clung to it. Then the flood was over his head, and he was blinded, buffeted, whirled along in water so icy-cold that he soon lost all sense of feeling, and only kept hold of Renti's mane because his hand seemed to be frozen fast to the lock of hair.

Many years afterwards, when he was trying to tell his children and grand-children what happened in the flooded river, he would say that he couldn't be sure it wasn't all a dream. He remembers opening his eyes and seeing fish whirling and circling in thousands, their silver sides flashing and darkening as they moved, turning and twisting as if they were all pulled by the same thread. And among them two huge fish, twining and spiralling together like two strands of rope, their jaws open showing the terrible teeth, their breath spraying up to the surface in bubbles of pearl. It was they who had dragged him down; he could see the torn cloth of his trouser-leg trailing from one wicked jaw. They turned, still twining together, to seize him again. The great mouths gaped; the teeth glistened; bubbles rose in a thick cloud like frog-spawn. Then suddenly, just as they were about to grab him, they were shouldered aside by a flock of sleek, beautiful creatures which sounded from Ludo's description like dolphins; but by this time I think the boy must have been close to losing his senses, because, as you know, dolphins live in the sea, and besides, they aren't fish at all, but animals like you and me. And certainly Ludo must have been dreaming when he talked later of 'an old man, sitting on the gravel at the bottom of the river, with his beard floating out on the current, and his hands full of blue stones, and a spear beside him'. The old man, says Ludo, seemed as much at home under the water as the fish did, and you and I know that, whatever the fairy-stories say, that simply can't be true.

Anyway, says Ludo, the old man suddenly looked up and saw them, boy and horse, whirling past in the flood, and he dropped the blue stones and reached for the spear. His eyes were very blue and very cold, as cold as the water. But even though he was at home under the water, he moved slowly, as ordinary people do when they are diving. He grasped the spear with his pale, knotted hand, but before he could raise it and strike at Ludo, the water between them suddenly boiled and darkened, and Ludo and Renti were swept violently downstream out of the old man's reach, and at the same time they were flung to the surface, and could breathe …

Only afterwards did Ludo know what had happened. High up above the rocks behind them, where the rain had poured down so hard as to melt the great masses of snow into new streams, these streams, flooding down too suddenly and too fast, like jets from an enormous water-pot, had torn a hole in the rocks and poured through in a new, rushing deluge. This came tearing down through the rocks, gathering more and more force as it came, with boulders and stones and gravel and the perishingly cold meltwater of the high snows and, like a huge wave breaking, it struck the main river and came roaring down the river-bed like a tidal wave three metres high, and swept Ludo and Renti clear out of the terrible Fishes' Pool and straight on down the gorge to where, like a sharp horizon, was a broad edge of rock over which the river fell in a mist of roaring spray, into a deep pool nearly ten metres below.

It was worse than any avalanche. It was choking, blinding, buffeting, but by this time Ludo was so cold and so bemused with the noise and the bruising from stones and the sharp rocks he was dragged over that he felt nothing at all except the awful sensation of not being able to breathe. But he still did by instinct the only sensible thing, which was to hold on tightly to Renti's mane. And though Renti hadn't had, any more than Ludo, any chance to learn to swim, all animals except man know this by instinct. So as soon as boy and horse plunged over the fall into the deep pool below, and came kicking to the surface, old Renti struck out gallantly, dragging Ludo with him. All of a sudden Ludo felt himself being dragged over gravel, then over grass – then he was lying on the river's bank, with water pouring out of his mouth and lungs, and breathing the lovely air again, safe.

He lay there for quite a long time doing very little more than come back to life, before he raised his head to look around him.

And saw, carved into a clay bank where a king-fisher was making a hole for her nest, the sign: ♈ The Water-Carrier had helped them, just as he had promised. Dangerous though it had been, he had washed Ludo and Renti safely through the House of the Fish, and into the House of the Ram.

And it was spring, and the rain had stopped, and the sun was shining.

CHAPTER TEN

The Ram

From where Ludo was lying, all he could see was a green meadow full of flowers that stretched from the river's edge as far as the eye could reach. The grass was young and golden-green, and hazed over with all the colours of springing meadow-flowers. Daisies, buttercups, cuckoo-flowers, violets, all the shades of white and gold and lilac, and everywhere among them, most vivid of all, the blazing blue bells of the gentians. The sky swarmed with singing larks. Ludo lay for a long while just enjoying the warmth of the sun, and recovering from his journey through the

House of the Fish. He had been so badly shaken that for the time being he had forgotten all about the need for haste, and Renti, for his part, seemed to have forgotten it, too. He was behaving like a foal, rolling over and over in the deep grass, till his coat was dry and clean again, and when at last he lumbered to his feet there were daisies tangled in his coat, and a swatch of buttercups caught up in his mane. He shook his neck, snorted with pleasure, and began to eat.

This reminded Ludo that he, too, was hungry, and that there was nothing left but a small heel of bread. He sat up, and looked around him.

It was a strange field. I suppose it might be more accurate to call it a prairie, for the rolling grass stretched for a mile or more to the horizon, where trees stood up against the sky. Towards these trees, now, the sun was sloping, touching their crests with brilliant gold. Nearer at hand one solitary tree stood alone, casting a patch of shade on the grass. It was rather a strange tree. Ludo could see the young leaves opening green all along its boughs, among the blossom, but there were still apples clinging there, round and glossy and yellow as gold, as fresh as the blossom and the buds of spring. They looked delicious.

Ludo got up and approached the tree. Its trunk was so old and writhen that it looked for all the world as if a dragon was sleeping, wreathed tightly round it. The best apples, as they always are, were at the very top, but there were some quite eatable ones hanging well within reach, and for one of these he put out a hand.

Then jumped, startled, as a voice said from the tree: 'If you steal my apples, you will turn into stone, and die.'

Ludo looked round him in alarm, but could see nobody. Then he saw an eye regarding him from the middle of the tree-trunk, and he saw that there *was* a dragon curled round the tree, close, like a thick stem of ivy, with his old, wicked head laid flat along the stump of a branch, and one red eye open just a slit, watching Ludo.

Ludo jumped away from that tree as fast as if the apple had bitten him, and the dragon laughed. 'Ho, ho,' it said, and the sound was like the rattling of twigs in the wind.

Another voice spoke from above, in a hoarse whisper. 'Don't take any notice of him, fledgling. If you eat one of my apples, you will turn into gold, and stay young for ever and ever.'

Ludo looked up. Above him on a high branch of the tree, regarding him with her enormous round eyes, was a brown owl.

Ludo looked from one to the other. 'Whose tree is it?' he asked nervously.

'Mine,' said the dragon, rattling his scales.

'Mine,' said the owl, turning her head very rapidly right round till she was looking the other way, then back again to stare at Ludo, and repeating this till he felt quite dizzy.

'Is there anything to eat besides the apples?'

'No,' said the dragon, 'nothing at all.'

'No,' said the owl, 'nothing of any description whatsoever.'

'Then what do you eat?' asked Ludo. He was growing a little bolder, because the dragon hadn't moved from the tree-trunk, and really seemed so very slow and old; and the owl was fat and fluffy and rather cuddly, and didn't look as if she ever harmed anything. Which only shows how wrong it is to judge by appearances.

'Oh,' said the dragon, in a slow gentle voice, 'a few leaves sometimes, or a bite or two of dry grass that nobody else wants … Not very much. You see, I'm so old and slow that by the time I climb off my tree the others have eaten everything up.'

'Others?'

'Those sweet creatures,' said the dragon. 'Bless them, why *shouldn't* they take the best of everything?' And a tear squeezed from the red eye.

Ludo looked round and saw that there were sheep feeding in the field, and a lot of them had lambs, very young and white and frisky. None of them were anywhere near the tree, and even the lambs were playing King-of-the-Castle at the very far side of the field.

'Dear little things,' said the dragon. 'So young and innocent, and so very tender … Of course, if you were just to pick one of my apples, not to eat it, you know, but just to offer it to one of those poor, sweet, hungry young lambs —'

'But if it would turn them into stone and kill them,' said Ludo, 'I don't think that would be a very nice thing to do.'

'Oh, that was only my fun,' said the dragon, rattling like a reed-bed in the wind. 'Only my fun. It wouldn't do the least bit of harm in the world. Not the least bit of harm. Just pick an apple, and call the lamb over here … or more than one lamb, if you like. Several lambs, in fact.' And from the corner of its long, long mouth a drop of saliva drooled down the tree trunk to the ground.

'No, no,' said the owl sharply from overhead. 'Don't bother the lambs, you'd only be wasting your time. Now if you would pick one of my apples, any one, it doesn't matter, and just lay it down on the ground in the shade of the tree, so that the field-mice could get it … ? Poor little things, I see them running about out there in the sunshine, with nothing at all to eat but a few dry roots and seeds.'

And indeed Ludo could see them, scuttling here

and there in the sunny grass, but never, never coming near the tree.

Now Ludo had never met a dragon before, but he had seen plenty of owls, and he knew quite well that owls, however well-spoken, ate field-mice whenever they could get hold of them. So it was a safe guess that, like the owl, the dragon was deceiving him, and ate lambs.

He said, very politely: 'I don't think I'd better do that, sir and ma'am. But if you'd either of you care for a bite of bread, I think there's a bit left.'

And he walked forward into the shade of the tree.

Three things happened at once.

The owl shrieked: 'Hoo! He's mine!' and flew down out of the tree to fasten her claws in Ludo's collar.

The dragon hissed: 'Ho! He's mine!' and, with his scales rattling till the tree shook, slid down the trunk all in one shimmering movement, and grabbed Ludo's trouser-leg.

A new voice roared: *'No! Mine!'* And past Ludo came a huge shape – four thundering hoofs and a heavy body fleeced with gold and two great horns curled round and round on themselves like snail-shells – and the biggest ram Ludo had ever seen flashed past him and went *SLAM* into the trunk of the tree, missing the dragon's tail by a centimetre, and bringing a shower of apples down which struck dragon, owl and Ludo with a positive hail of golden fruit as heavy and hard as cannon balls. The dragon said a very bad word indeed, let go Ludo's leg, and swarmed back up the tree and hung there, panting, its long forked tongue flickering and the red eyes shifting nervously. The owl, who was a lady even in moments of stress, said 'Sorry, I'm sure,' and flew back to her bough with a few feathers floating off her, and sat twisting her head round and back, round and back, and not meeting anyone's eye.

The Ram withdrew from the tree, shook his head slightly (though the blow didn't seem to have hurt him at all), and regarded Ludo.

'Well, boy?' he asked.

Ludo knew, of course, who he was; the Ram himself, the lord of the House. What he did not know was that this was Chrysomallion, the great Ram whose golden fleece was one day to be the prize in another adventure. Or perhaps it had been the prize in that adventure hundreds of years ago? There's no telling, because there is no time, as we understand it, in the star country where Ludo was travelling. But the Ram was enormous, and majestic and very beautiful; he also had a brow as broad as a shield and as hard as a battering-ram (which was called after him); and he could have knocked Ludo flying clean back into the Fishes'

Pool with one blow. So Ludo stood respectfully in front of the Ram, trying not to rub his leg where the dragon's grip had burned a hole in his trousers, and said:

'If you please, your worship, I'm Ludo, and I'm taking my horse Renti along the track to catch up with the sun.'

The Ram stood with his head slightly lowered, and appeared to be thinking. His eyes were as yellow as Goat's, but not so cold. If you thought very hard about it, you could still see, in this majestic creature, the young golden lamb he must once have been, skipping like the others in the sunshine among the daisies. (But the black Goat could never, never have been young, thought Ludo.)

'And you would crave my leave to pass unmolested through my House?' said the Ram gravely.

Ludo wouldn't have thought of putting it like that, but it sounded better than, 'Please let me go and don't hurt me,' so he said, 'Yes, sir, please, sir,' and rubbed his leg.

'What ails your leg?' asked the Ram.

'It's a bit burned. Nothing to mention, sir,' said Ludo.

'Come here.'

Ludo obeyed him. The Ram lowered his splendid head and breathed on the sore leg, and it was like a cool bandage being wrapped round it. The soreness vanished and the reddened flesh smoothed and looked as good as new.

'Oh, thank you,' said Ludo. 'Thank you very much.'

'And now,' said the Ram, 'if you desire an apple, take it. It will do you no harm at all. And take one for your horse. But only one each.'

Ludo thanked him again, and picked two of the fallen ones off the ground.

The Ram watched him. 'Why did you pick those up? The ones still on the tree are better.'

'These are quite good enough for me and Renti, thank you. I've still got a bit of bread. You rescued me before they got that.'

While Ludo had been talking to the Ram, Renti, who had looked up from his grazing at the crash when the Ram struck the tree, now came limping over to Ludo's side. The buttercups still hung in his mane, but he had eaten most of the daisies. (No animal likes buttercups, which explains why the fields are always so full of them.) He chewed the daisies quickly and swallowed them, and reached his neck out for an apple. Ludo gave him one, then broke the heel of bread carefully in two, and handed him that as well. The Ram watched gravely.

Then, because it looked as if the Ram expected him to eat the apple straight away, like Renti, he bit into it. It was delicious, not like any apple he had ever tasted before. It had the apple-taste, but along with that came flavours, different with each bite, of other fruits; peaches, pineapples, apricots, pears, nectarines, fat juicy grapes ... Ludo finished the apple, core and all, and wiped his mouth, feeling a whole lot better.

'That was the nicest apple I ever tasted,' he told the Ram, who looked pleased.

'It will assuage your hunger for the nonce,' he said.

'Yes, sir, your worship,' said Ludo uncertainly.

A tiny glint appeared in the Ram's grave golden eyes; a glint that belonged to the lamb he must once have been. 'I meant,' he said, 'that it will keep you going for a bit. They'll probably give you something better in the next House. They always seem to be feasting, there.'

Ludo remembered what Gula had said: 'Feast one man and kill the next as soon as look at him.' But he said nothing, for the Ram was going on:

'I doubt if you will catch the sun in the next House, but you should be on your way very soon. He is harnessing his horses back already, and soon he will be gone.'

'You mean he is *here*?' Ludo stared around him eagerly. Then he noticed something he had not noticed before; the tracks of two wheels running

straight across the prairie as far as the horizon,
with between them the flurry of crushed grasses
where the sun's four horses had galloped. The
tracks ran clear up to the trees on the horizon, and
even as he watched, his eyes narrow against the
brightness, he saw rays, brilliant and almost level,
shoot out along the turf as the sun came out from
behind the trees and moved along the sky's edge in
a blaze of gold.

His heart lifted, for he knew that he must be nearer
than he had ever been before. In the heart of that
blaze he had caught a glimpse of the chariot and the
sparkling manes and the whip like the flash of light
along a cobweb.

His heart was beating hard, but he stood still and
asked the Ram: 'May I follow him, sir?'

'You may. I shall not harm you. I have never
harmed anything young. But whether your old horse
can catch him is another matter.'

'Sir,' said Ludo, 'would you breathe on my horse's
leg, too, and heal him?'

The Ram shook his handsome head. 'He will be
healed when it is time. This is the House of the
Young. Now go quickly, boy, and go warily.'

He turned and trotted away towards the sheep on
the other side of the pasture. The sheep stopped their
grazing to watch him, and the lambs came skipping
down from the knolls where they had been playing,

and jumped and frisked towards him.

Ludo grabbed Renti's halter and pulled his head up from the grass, saying breathlessly: 'Come on, Renti! Quickly, old horse, we're closer by miles! Come as fast as you can!'

Renti threw his head up and whinnied, as if the excitement was catching. He broke into an uneven trot beside Ludo, and they both ran across the grass in the track of the chariot's wheels. As they ran Ludo caught a glimpse of the great Ram, in the midst of the flock of white and golden lambs, busily playing King-of-the-Castle. He was poised on top of a flowery knoll, with the lambs bouncing and frisking all round him. Then a very small lamb jumped up beside him and gave him a push easily strong enough to dislodge a butterfly from a flower, and golden Chrysomallion leaped down, to be overwhelmed by the crowd of lambs skipping and jostling like boiling soapsuds.

When Ludo and Renti, both breathless, had reached the trees, the sun was out of sight. There was a gate across the way, but the marks of the wheels went on on the other side, so Ludo pushed the gate open, and shut it again after Renti, without noticing the sign on it which said:

♉ BEWARE OF THE BULL

But a second later, when he turned to go on, he saw the Bull himself, standing squarely in the middle of the track, with his horns lowered and ready, and one hoof tearing up the turf in front of him.

CHAPTER ELEVEN

The Bull

Now as I have told you, Ludo used to go every summer up to the summer farm, and help mind the cows while his father made cheeses. They had bulls up there, too, so Ludo was used to cattle, and knew quite a lot about them. He was not really afraid of bulls, but, like everyone who deals with them, he respected them, and he never, never made the mistake of trusting one, however friendly he looked. And this one did not look friendly at all. When a bull starts pawing at the ground with his forehoof, it is time to be very careful indeed.

Ludo knew that the one thing it would be fatal to do, would be to run away, or even to move at all. The only thing to do when faced at close quarters by an angry bull is to stand quite still.

He stood quite still.

He stood quite still for so long that he was afraid he was going to sneeze.

Beside him Renti, who was not afraid of the bull, but was rather anxious not to draw its attention to himself, stood quite still too.

The Bull – for of course it was the Bull himself – stopped pawing at the ground, and stood quite still.

And there they all might be standing to this day, but they were interrupted. Two little girls, about the same age as Ludo, came running out of the trees. They had been picking flowers, and between them they held a daisy chain as thick as a skipping rope.

Before Ludo could move or shout a warning, they ran straight up to the Bull and flung the daisy chain round his massive neck. The Bull lowered his head even further, so that his horns looked wider than ever. His huge eyes rolled, showing the whites, and then, to Ludo's amazement, he asked in a low voice:

'What is it? It's been standing there without saying a word, without moving even, for ages and ages.'

The little girls stood, one on each side of the Bull, holding the ends of the daisy chain. They both stared at Ludo. They were not like any girls he had seen before. They were dainty and finely made, like porcelain figures, and they had dresses on which looked as if they were made of flowers. Nothing else but flowers, with perhaps a bit of ribbon here and there to hold them together. What was more, they had wings. At first Ludo hardly recognised these as wings; they were tiny, just plumes of feathers growing from their shoulders, white and soft like the wings of doves – and no bigger. In fact, as wings, they were quite useless. They would never have allowed even these dainty little girls to fly, any more than would the tiny wings that Ludo had seen on the paintings of cherubs in church at home. But these girls were not like any cherubs he had seen; certainly not like angels. And not a bit like fairies, either. But whatever they were, Ludo knew they were beings far superior to a poor peasant boy, so he stood there shyly, in silence, till one of them should speak to him.

But they spoke only to the Bull. One of them bent down to whisper in its ear: 'I think it's a faun.'

'I don't think it can be a faun,' said the Bull, still in that low voice, as if he didn't want Ludo to hear. 'It's such a strange shape, and besides, it has fur right up to its neck. Fauns are bare to the waist. And its feet are wrong, and its ears – fauns have pointed ears, and this one hasn't any ears that I can see.'

'They're probably under its hair,' said one of the

little girls, who obviously took Ludo's woollen cap for hair, just as the Bull had been mistaken about his coat. ('As if anyone had bright blue hair, or fur with buttons on,' thought Ludo, but not very clearly, for he was still a little frightened, and very much puzzled.)

'I don't think it has any ears at all,' whispered the Bull. 'It obviously can't hear a word we say.'

'It's a foreign faun, I think,' said the other little girl. 'It doesn't understand.'

'But it must be blind, too,' said the Bull, sounding worried. 'It's stood there without moving or speaking for about an hour and a half.'

Now in fact Ludo had stood there for only about two minutes – which seemed an age when one was, not frightened exactly, but rather nervous – but most bulls tend to exaggerate a little. This is why you can't rely on them. But it didn't seem as if this Bull were unfriendly, so Ludo took a breath to give himself courage, and said: 'If you please, sir —'

'It does talk!' cried one of the little girls, the one whose dress was tied up with forgetmenots.

'And it isn't foreign!' cried the other, who was dressed in wild roses. 'It must just have come through the wood from the House of the Ram. What are you, then?' she demanded. 'If you're not a faun, and you're not a satyr, and you're not one of the tree people or the water people, then what are you, and why did the Ram let you through?'

'Please, I'm a boy,' began Ludo, but then his words were drowned in a burst of music, a great fanfare of trumpets and flutes and all sorts of instruments that he didn't recognise. The Bull threw up his head, and the little girls, swinging on the wide horns, cried out: 'Oh, it's time for the feast! We'd better hurry! You, faun, boy, whatever you call yourself, you can come too, if you want! Come quickly now, or you'll miss the singing! Here, catch!'

The forgetmenot girl flung him the end of the daisy chain. Ludo caught it, and when the Bull, without another glance at him, moved off in stately fashion towards the trees, with the little girls skipping along beside him, Ludo followed.

Renti was already eating greedily, cropping the fresh grass and flowers. Ludo thought, rather enviously, that it seemed a very long time since breakfast, with nothing but an apple, even though that apple came from a magic tree; but perhaps after the singing there might be food for him, too? He ran forward, and when the Bull reached the crest of the bank Ludo was just beside him, and could look down into the hollow beyond.

This was nearly circular, with a round pool in its centre. All round the edge of the pool were irises, yellow and purple and white, with leaves sticking up like spears. On the water were water lilies, but not like the ones Ludo knew; these had enormous leaves, quite round, with the edges turned up like pie-crust; the lilies themselves were blue, standing up above the surface of the water. On the lily-leaves there were frogs sitting, and long-legged birds which stepped daintily from one leaf to the next as if they were stepping-stones. But strangest of all, some little girls like the two who were with the Bull were sitting there, too, each one right in the middle of a lily-leaf, cross-legged and playing a flute or a trumpet or a lyre or some musical instrument that Ludo had never heard of. All the time they played their tiny wings vibrated like the wings of bees, so fast that they were visible only as a gossamer blur. If Ludo had had time to think at all, he might have thought that the wings were keeping girls, leaves and all from sinking.

But he didn't stop to think about it; he was only thinking about the food which he could not only smell, but see. Half-way down the bank between him and the pool there was a fire burning, and over this a kind of gridiron, a grill standing on four legs like a table. On this was a huge cauldron from which came the most appetising smell, and on the grass near the fire was dish after dish of fruit and big crusty loaves ready buttered, and apple turnovers and sausage rolls and crumpets dripping with butter and bowls of strawberries with whipped cream piled on top, and jellies the shape (and very nearly the size) of castles, in glowing reds and greens and yellows, with little flecks of gold in them like the snow in one of those glass globes that hold a snowstorm.

'Come *on*!' cried the little girls, and danced downhill with the Bull trotting after them, and Ludo running happily after the Bull.

What a feast that was! There was more than enough for everyone, though when Ludo reached the fire he found that the place was crowded, for all that he hadn't seen anybody arriving. One moment there was just the empty green hollow full of sunlight, with nothing but the trees surrounding it, and the water glittering, and the winged sprites balancing on the lily-leaves making their music; then suddenly the place was full of people dancing and singing and feasting and laughing. There were real fauns, which are like boys to the waist down, but below that they have hairy flanks like young goats, and little tails. They have horns, too, half hidden in their shaggy hair. They were as agile as goats, and leaped and skipped about, eating greedily and laughing with their mouths full. They looked gay and friendly, but their eyes were the same cold yellow as the great Goat of Capricorn, so Ludo kept away from them. He felt safer with the girls who were chattering all the time, and were dressed in flowers; and with the green people who spoke in whispers and were dressed in leaves; and with the strange dumb people who didn't eat at all, but drank a lot and looked as if they were clothed only in flowing water. In the midst of all this moving, feasting crowd the Bull stood munching the daisy chain, looking much like any ordinary bull, only bigger and grander. He appeared to have forgotten all about Ludo, who sat quietly without anyone taking much notice of him, and ate and ate of the gorgeous food, rather greedily perhaps, but, 'Who knows,' thought Ludo, 'when I'll get a chance to eat again? And it's the Twins after this, and the Crab … They're not likely to give me anything to eat. Eat me themselves, more likely.' But even this thought couldn't depress him, because the food was so lovely and the music so beautiful and the dancing throng around him so friendly, and all the warmth and richness of summer seemed contained in that hollow under the summer sun.

Presently he had finished, and lay back on the warm grass, watching as the strange people danced. After a while he heard the little girls calling out: 'Now the Game! The Bull-game!' And the one with the forgetmenots started looking round her, and Ludo heard her say:

'We can start with the foreign boy. He can play Catch first.'

Now if there was one thing Ludo didn't want to do, it was play Catch with a bull chasing him, so before the little girl could see him he got quietly to his feet and crept up the bank again, and lay flat there in the long grass, with his chin on his hands, watching the frolics below.

They soon gave up looking for him, and the game began. Everybody knows the game; it was just a version of Tig – a sort of mixture of it and Hide and Seek and Blind Man's Buff. The Bull was It, and the object of the game seemed to be to run in and throw chains of flowers round his horns and neck without letting him touch you. They all seemed very quick at it, and the Bull didn't touch anyone, so Ludo got no chance to see what happened if anyone got caught. The game went on for what seemed a very long time. The sun slanted lower, and Ludo watched it, remembering that he must wait until dark before going farther along the track into the House of the Twins. Finally he realised that the laughter had grown less, and that the game was over. He looked down. The Bull was standing stock-still in the midst of the crowd, almost hidden by the twining chains of poppies and meadowsweet and purple columbines and all the flowers of high summer. He stood quite still, as still as when Ludo had first seen him. If you hadn't known that the chains which bound him were only flowers, still full of scent and freshness, and with the bees and butterflies still busy over them, you would have thought he was bound too fast to move.

As the Bull stood there, the girls and the tree-people and the water-people and the fauns joined hands and began to pace solemnly round him, singing. And this song was different from the others; it was slower and graver, but even more joyous. Birds were coming out of the trees now, to circle above the dancers, adding their own songs. From the boughs above the bank where Ludo lay came a flock of white doves, floating downhill with wings raked back, like a shower of white petals.

At that moment Ludo realised that Renti was no longer near him. He sat up abruptly and looked around him. The old horse was nowhere to be seen. Ludo jumped to his feet, and then saw, a long way across the grass, the horse busily grazing where rushes and yellow irises marked the bank of a distant stream. Beyond the stream there was no grass, only a steep track winding up between rocks. It looked like quite a different country.

A different country … The Badlands! Ludo shouted in sudden panic: 'Renti, Renti, come back!' But Renti, unheeding, forged forward through the splashing stream and started away up the track.

Dimly, Ludo was aware that below him in the hollow the singing had stopped. Everyone was staring his way. Then, as if a strong wind had blown through the hollow, everything changed. The sprites on the lily-leaves faded into nothing, blowing away down the wind like petals. The leaf people stood quite still, with only their leaves flickering, and Ludo saw now that they were only trees, young trees, swaying in the wind. The water people shimmered, and gleamed iridescent and transparent as bubbles, then vanished. Even the little girls ran away and disappeared into the woods beyond the pool. From the shoulders and flanks of the Bull the flowers fell, fading, to lie in heaps round his feet. He lifted his splendid head and stared at Ludo with his huge, dark eyes.

From somewhere beyond the tree-tops came the first distant growl of thunder. Renti was out of sight. Ludo forgot all about standing quite still when a bull was watching you. He forgot all about staying in the House of the Bull until after dark. He turned and ran, just as hard as he could, after Renti.

'*Renti! Renti! Come back*!'

And behind him, as he ran, he heard a new and different thunder coming fast over the grass. The Bull was charging after him.

Ludo reached the stream. There was no sign of Renti. The Bull was still coming, faster than ever. The ground seemed to shake. Thunder in the ground, and thunder crashing, now, in the air. A whip of white lightning struck down into the water of the stream. As quickly and lightly as any of the winged people, Ludo leaped the stream and ran on, up the winding track, slipping and stumbling on the stones, till he reached the summit of the track, where it led between enormous cairns of dry rock.

Under his feet a stone slid, rolled, and twisted, and he fell flat on the path. He was not hurt, but he was shaken, and rather winded. For a full three or four seconds he lay there, before he could pull himself together and get to his feet again. As he picked himself up slowly, rubbing a sore knee, he realised that there was no longer any sound at all. The thunder had gone. There was no sign of the Bull. He looked back. Behind him the stream, the meadow, the whole landscape of summer was as distant as a dream.

There was no going back. He had to go on. And the sun was still high and bright, and he was in the House of the Twins where the Far-Shooter roamed.

Indeed, at that moment he saw the sign carved on a flat slab of rock beside him: And just beside it a notice standing which said:

 ⊓ FIRING RANGE. SHOOTING PRACTICE
   HERE DAILY. DO NOT ENTER

Beyond the notice was a flat, rocky plateau broken here and there by cairns of stone piled up higher than a man's head. Between two of these Renti was standing, with his ears laid flat back and the whites of his eyes showing. A man held him fast by the halter, while another stooped to examine his feet one by one, and a third –

The third man stood apart, on a tall rock, carefully fitting an arrow to his bow.

CHAPTER TWELVE

The Twins

The man who was examining Renti's feet looked up, saw Ludo, and said something to the other. The two of them were exactly alike. Ludo remembered, in one awful flash, all that Gula had told him about the Twins and the terrible Far-Shooter. Now, because Renti knew no better, they had come into the House of the Twins by daylight, and they were caught.

Ludo was only a boy, and in that first moment of panic fear I think he might even have left Renti where he was, and have turned and run away, but the man on the rock, who must be the Far-Shooter, had seen him, too. He swung the great bow round and pointed the arrow straight at Ludo.

Ludo stood still. He remembered what the Archer had said to him: 'This horse served you faithfully all through his life; now will you serve him and keep faith with him?' Confusedly, he wondered if keeping faith with Renti might mean being killed along with him. But it seemed he hadn't much choice. The Far-Shooter's arrow could reach him before he ran two steps. Something else came into his mind, Gula telling him, 'Talk first and fight afterwards is a good motto.'

So Ludo, though he was frightened, stood his ground much as he had stood it in front of the Bull, and when it was apparent that he was not going to run away, the Far-Shooter lowered the great golden bow.

The Twin who had first seen Ludo strode right up to him and stood over him, bending his thick neck to stare down at the boy. He was a very handsome man, broad and strong, with thick curling black hair, and black eyes set close under thick brows which met in the middle. The hair grew low on his forehead, and his nose was short and straight with wide nostrils. He looked, in fact, rather like the Bull, all beef and not much brain, but that was no comfort to Ludo, who had been hoping to talk these men out of doing him or Renti any harm.

The Twin did not waste any time on greetings or

courtesies. 'Who said you could come through our land?' he demanded.

'Nobody, please, sir,' said Ludo. 'But I was following the track, and I was told I had to come this way. The Archer told us to follow the sun, you see. I'm sorry if I'm trespassing, but my horse strayed, and I came to get him back. I – I hope he hasn't done any damage?'

The Twin scowled down at him for a few moments without speaking, almost as if he couldn't understand what Ludo was saying. Then he reached his big hand out and jerked Peleus' knife from the boy's belt.

'We'll have this, for a start. Coming armed. Threatening us. Can't have that, can we? Got to defend ourselves.'

'Oh, no,' said Ludo eagerly, 'I wouldn't dream of threatening anyone. Peleus gave me the knife, and Gula – the Water-Carrier, you know – he said —'

'Not that I couldn't truss you up with one hand, knife or no knife,' said the Twin, who wasn't listening. He was trying the edge of Peleus' knife with his thumb, and beginning to smile. It was not a smile that Ludo liked at all. 'Truss you up with one hand tied behind my back, I could, and eat you for breakfast.'

'Of course you could, sir,' said Ludo, hoping to placate him. 'I couldn't harm you, not possibly. If you'd just let us go on after the sun, we'd be out of your land in just a few minutes, and no harm done.

Or if there's any work I could do to pay you —'

'Harm us?' exclaimed the Twin. 'I'd like to see you try! Just try! You'd see soon enough where you'd get to! Take you apart in the twinkling of an eye, I could.'

And as he spoke his free hand shot out, and he seized Ludo by the shoulder.

At that moment he was interrupted. The other Twin, who was still holding Renti's halter, shouted out: 'Castor! Bring him over here! Lykeios wants to speak to him.'

Castor, gripping Ludo's shoulder more tightly than ever, stopped smiling and looked disappointed, but to Ludo's surprise he made no attempt to argue. He gave Ludo a shake, and started to march him across the flat rocky ground towards the others. He grumbled a bit below his breath, but softly, Ludo noticed, so that the Far-Shooter (whose name seemed to be Lykeios) would not be able to hear him. Ludo did not try to break away – it would have done no good – but went with him quietly, hoping that Lykeios would be easier to talk to than Castor. The Twin, hustling him along, looked down with a sneer on his handsome face, and said: 'No fight in you, eh? Don't know what the young are coming to. When Pollux and I were your age we'd have been straight at it, knives, teeth, anything, as soon as look at you.'

'That's true,' said the other twin, as they came up to him. 'Take on anything, we would, up to eight times our size. Yes, and kill it, too.'

'Eight times?' said Castor. 'Ten times! Twenty times, I dare say, we've tackled in our time. Remember Amycus? Remember Idas? Now *there* was a fight.' And they both laughed heartily, but Castor kept his grip on Ludo's shoulder, while Pollux, who had finished examining Renti, still held tightly to the halter. But they made no attempt to hurt either the boy or the horse. They waited for Lykeios the Far-Shooter, who had come down from the high rock, and was approaching across the level ground.

Even through his fear, Ludo couldn't help thinking that he had never in all his life seen a man who looked like this man. He took long strides which seemed to skim the ground rather than tread on it, so that he moved forward with very little effort, and at great speed. It was like watching someone skating over dry rock. He was very tall, towering a full head over the Twins, and he was as fair as they were dark, with long thick hair falling like a heavy mane to his shoulders, and eyes of a brilliant pale blue. He was dressed in a short tunic-like garment of yellow, with a wolf-skin slung over his right shoulder. There was a quiver full of arrows at his hip; some were fledged with white goose feathers, and some with grey, and they were as long as a man's arm. The great bow which he carried was golden, with a double curve, and a golden bowstring which hummed by itself as he moved. At his heels ran his wolves, weaving to and fro, panting with lolling tongues and eyes fixed on Renti and Ludo. But they stayed behind their master.

Ludo was afraid of the Twins, as one might be afraid of quarrelsome bullies who were too stupid to do anything but hurt people smaller than themselves, but he was afraid of Lykeios the Far-Shooter with a fear that was half awe and half admiration, as one might fear a thunderstorm or a volcano.

Lykeios spoke, and his voice was musical but bloodless, like a trumpet.

'Leave them.'

The Twins obeyed. Castor's hand dropped from Ludo's shoulder, and Pollux let go the horse's halter. Ludo reached for the rope, and stood his ground between the two of them, holding Renti.

Pollux shuffled his feet in the dust. 'What is it, Lykeios? Let us do it for you. Not worth your trouble, they're not.'

'Waste of your arrows,' said Castor quickly. 'We'll do it as soon as look at you. Just say the word. Done in a trice.'

'It would be a kindness, come to think of it,' put in Pollux, not sounding kind at all, but rather eager. 'Because if the poor things managed to get away from us, the Crab would get them, and you know what *that* means.'

'Nevertheless,' said the Far-Shooter, 'you will

leave them to me.' He bent that stern terrible gaze on Ludo. He was only standing three paces off, but Ludo had the impression that he was being examined from somewhere as far away as the stars. He had to try three times before he could make a sound.

'Lord, your worship,' he began, licking his dry lips, 'we came from home only yesterday, and we're following the path of the sun. Renti – this is Renti, your honour – he fell in a snowdrift, and the only way out was through the cave where your brother lives. The Archer ... he is your brother, isn't he?'

'He is. He let you both through?'

'It was he who told us to follow the sun,' said Ludo; then, still stammering a little with nervousness, he went on to tell Lykeios about Renti's fall into the crevasse, about the Archer's advice, and about their journey. His story was not made any easier to tell by the Twins, who stood one on either side of him, fidgeting. Castor was sliding his thumb along the blade of Peleus' knife again, and muttering: 'Kill them quick as a flash, no trouble at all. But no fun. No fight in him. A peasant.' And on the other side of him Pollux nodded, agreeing. 'No sport in it at all. What does the Archer mean, letting a peasant boy through? Horse no use either. Lame as a duck. Sitting shot.'

The Far-Shooter said nothing, but listened with his eyes fixed on Ludo, standing so still that the boy began to think he wasn't listening, either. He stammered a bit more, floundering, then bit his tongue in his embarrassment, and stopped.

'There you are,' said Pollux immediately. 'Can't even talk straight. Useless. Give him to us, Wolf-lord. We'll reason with him.'

'Only one way to reason,' said Castor, running his thumb along the knife-blade, and grinning.

Lykeios took no notice of them at all. Ludo found it difficult even to look at him now. The sun was setting fast; it was right down on the horizon in a blaze of fire, and against it Lykeios was visible only as a looming shadow. The gold of his hair and the gold of the bow shimmered against the blaze. The rest was shadow. All that could be seen of the wolves was the glint of their watching eyes.

When he spoke his voice was fainter, as if it came from farther off. 'Boy,' he said, and the bowstring hummed as he spoke, 'when were you born?'

'Eleven years ago, sir,' said Ludo, surprised, 'on the first day of June.'

'I thought so,' said Lykeios. The brilliant eyes gleamed for a moment in the sunset as he turned to the restless Twins. 'You will let him pass,' he told them. 'He is mine. You will give him back his knife, Castor; and you will neither of you lay hands on him.'

The Twins stared for a few moments as if they

could hardly believe what they had heard. Then they looked at one another across Ludo's head. Their stupid, handsome faces were blank with surprise and dismay.

'But, Lykeios —' began Pollux.

'But, Lykeios —' said Castor.

'Those are my orders,' said the tall man, and the bowstring hummed on a deep note.

Ludo took a deep breath. He did not understand what was happening, but he knew that the Far-Shooter could protect him against the Twins, so he spoke up boldly, though his heart was thumping. 'Lord —'

'Well, boy?'

'May we really go? Now?'

'You may go,' said Lykeios. 'You were born in this House, and under the sign of Apollo Lykeios the lord of the Wolves, the Far-Shooter, the protector of flocks and herds. You are mine, and you have served me faithfully. While you are here in this House no harm shall come to you. You may rest here until daylight, and then, when the sun is risen, you will pass safely through the House of the Crab. But your horse may not go with you. He is maimed, and no maimed creature, beast or man, passes out from my House.'

'Do you mean – do you mean you can heal him?' asked Ludo.

'Kill or heal, it is the same,' said the Wolf lord. 'Now stand aside. In a moment the light will be gone.'

He raised the great bow and notched an arrow to it. The fletching was grey, and the barb shone grey, like steel. The bowstring sang on a high, terrible note. The last rays of the sun flashed along it like drops of blood running.

Castor reluctantly handed over Peleus' knife, then he and Pollux moved aside as they had been told. But Ludo did not move away from Renti. The old horse was standing facing the Far-Shooter, head on, making a very narrow target for the arrow. Ludo nerved himself to stand still, as squarely as he could in front of the horse, between him and the arrow, and to plead with Lykeios for Renti's life.

'Lord —' he began.

'Stand aside,' said the Far-Shooter sternly, but just as he spoke the Twins, stupid to the last, walked across between him and Ludo. At the same moment the sun, dropping lower, sank behind the western horizon like a burning wheel plunging into water, flooding the sky with crimson, and sending long shadows shooting.

Ludo whipped round, quick as an eel, and flung himself on Renti's back. He dragged on the halter rope and kicked Renti in the ribs and shouted: 'Go on! *Quick, Renti, quick!*'

And Renti obeyed. He must have been as frightened as Ludo, because almost before the boy landed on his back he was galloping, lame foot and all, for the shelter of the nearest rocks.

Ludo, lying flat and hanging on like grim death to the horse's mane, heard the Twins shout, both together, one loud, angry yell. Then Lykeios' voice, calm and – incredibly – laughing:

'Leave them. Wait.'

Ludo, his cheek close to Renti's neck, turned his head to look. Already the rocky flatland was deep in shadow. The Twins stood together, shoulder to shoulder, like two squat pillars of rock. Beyond them, a shadow against the swimming crimson sky, the Far-Shooter towered, tall as a tree, tall as a crag, tall as the sky itself. The bow shone across the sky like a rainbow. There was no escaping it …

There was a sound like a plucked harp, and then with a ripple of music and a flash and a long whirr like the wind in a hawk's wing, an arrow fled past Ludo's cheek. A white goose feather brushed his face, the golden barb grazed Renti's neck, and the arrow fled past into the growing darkness. They never heard it strike.

Then they were engulfed by the shadow of the sheltering rocks, and galloping down a long straight stretch of track towards the sea.

CHAPTER THIRTEEN

The Crab

The beach was long and straight, so long that, in the gathering darkness, Ludo could not see what lay at the far end. On one hand lay the sea, low and ice-cold, with stars glinting along the grey reaches of the sky above the horizon. The grey clouds and the glinting stars seemed to be moving, racing along the sky as Renti raced along the beach. It was as if Lykeios' wolves ran with the galloping horse. Ludo thought he could hear the scrabble of their ghostly claws.

On the other hand the beach was bounded by high

black cliffs which reached as far as the eye could see. They towered like a giants' wall against the black sky where, slowly, the moon began to rise.

Ludo lay flat on Renti's neck and clung to the flying mane as the horse galloped, with no sign now of his lameness, along the flat smooth shore. Between the starlight and the growing moonlight he found he could see fairly clearly for a short distance ahead. He saw the sign of the Crab scrawled clear across the sand, looking like this: ♋

Then Renti galloped straight across it and the sand was scuffed and scattered, and the horse, with stretched neck and pricked ears, raced with the sea on one hand and the cliff on the other, along the narrow gauntlet of the beach.

There was nothing to be seen; no man, no beast, nothing except the sea shifting and whispering, with the moon staring white from the sky above the cliff, and on the flat dark sands a myriad of tiny crabs scuttling sideways from the fast, steady beat of Renti's hoofs.

'Renti,' whispered Ludo, 'Lykeios has helped us. Because I was born in his House; and because he's lord of flocks and herds and I've looked after them all my life; and because he hates the darkness. That arrow – he was going to kill you with the grey arrow, but he changed it and touched you with the white one, and you're healed. You're healed, Renti! You won't be lame any more! We can catch the sun chariot now …! There's nothing to stop us now! These silly little crabs, they can't do us any harm! And look, there's the end of the beach!'

Ludo found it hard to believe that the most dreaded of all his ordeals had been so easy. And he was right. Renti was just half-way along the beach, going as fast as he had ever gone in his life, even as a young horse, when something moved among the black rocks to their right.

The cliffs themselves were moving. Something huge, like a vast black boulder, reared itself up on its eight segmented legs as a mountain might suddenly rear itself straight off the ground on eight crazy pillars. There was the sound, a thousand times louder than any they had heard till now, of claws scraping on the icy rock. Two cold eyes glared out of the dark. Something spoke in a cold, dry, acid voice.

'Who dares to come through my House by night?'

There was no question here of parleying or waiting for the pleasure of the lord of the House. Ludo knew well what the Crab's pleasure would be. And so did Renti. With a snort of terror the old horse laid his ears flat once more and leaped into an even faster gallop than before.

But he had no more chance than a scurrying insect has when a spider pounces. The Crab lurched sideways, like a landslide, and one of the hinged claws lifted high across the moon. It was one of the pincer claws, and it was toothed like a shark, and open, and it stretched clean across the sky.

Then suddenly, through the dark, like the flash of lightning or a spear thrown white-hot, something whistled past Ludo's cheek. For a moment Ludo thought it was an arrow all of gold, then he saw the long train of sparks behind it, and knew it for what it was; a shooting star. It shot out of the far sky where the wolf-stars glared and the cold moon drifted. It struck the claw with a clang and a crack like a hammer striking glass. The claw broke. The Crab made a sound like the air going out of a huge bellows, and the cold eyes vanished. The landslide lurched the other way, back under the looming blackness of the cliffs, and settled into stillness. The beach was empty.

Ludo put his face down against Renti's hot neck, and shut his eyes.

'Lykeios, thank you. Thank you. Lord of the shooting stars, thank you.'

Then all around them were trees, with leaves shutting out the moonlight, and underfoot the sand gave way to the scented softness of a forest floor.

CHAPTER FOURTEEN

The Lion and the Lady

The night in the House of the Crab had been the worst that Ludo was ever to spend in his life, but it was also the shortest. As his horse paced gently forward through the forest trees the darkness began to lift, and soon, quite suddenly, like a great rosy lamp taking light, the sun came up, flooding everything with glory, and sending long shafts of red-gold between the tree-trunks where Renti walked.

The light showed a forest such as Ludo had never seen before. The forests of his home were vast and thickly crowded, mile on mile of pine woods

stretching right to the tops of the hills. At the forests'
edge, where the sun could reach, flowers grew; but
deep in the forests themselves nothing grew at all
except pale shapes of toadstools pushing through the
loam like witches' hats.

But this forest! You and I would have known it was
a tropical forest, and that Ludo was now very near the
sun; but Ludo had never heard of the tropics, and gaped
amazed from Renti's back as he looked about him.

To begin with, the trees were half as high again as
they were at home, and beneath them the growth of
tree-ferns and flowering bushes was so thick that you
couldn't see even halfway up the tallest trunks.
Creepers hung like ropes from bough to bough, some
of them with leaves as big as paddles, and great
scarlet or purple flowers shaped like trumpets or
huge starfish. Whole clusters of orchids sprouted
from the crotches of trees. Fireflies floated by like
clouds of sparks. The forest was rich with a sort of
steamy warmth, and heavy with all the scents you
can imagine. It was humming with cheerful bees all
stacking the honey away in their own secret combs
for their own use; and all a-whistle with birds
stuffing themselves with fruit and fat insect-grubs
and delicious caterpillars.

And when Ludo and Renti, dodging the hanging
flowers where humming-birds whirred and darted
and hung like flashing glass in the beams of the sun,

came at length to the end of the forest, they felt like swimmers emerging from a bathe in tropical water, heavy, warm, and a bit sticky. It was lovely to be out in the air and to feel the fresh scented breeze of a summer day and to hear, not too far ahead down a winding lane, the cool trickle of water.

Renti, with head up and ears pricked, and glossy coat shining like a new horse-chestnut in the sunlight, blew through his nostrils at the sound of the water, and trotted round the bend in the lane.

There was a well there, set back to one side of the lane, with a grassy lawn in front of it. The well was square, with a low, wide stone parapet. Behind it stood a big stone rather like a gravestone. There was carving on it. To one side was carved the sign: ♌ and to the other the sign: ♍

Under the second sign sat an old woman, dressed like the peasant women of Ludo's own country, with a hood over her head. She had beside her on the stone a big market-basket covered with a cloth, from beneath which peeped the leg of a cooked chicken, and a luscious-looking bunch of black grapes.

Under the other sign, stretched along the stone of the parapet as if it was a hearthrug, lay the biggest cat Ludo had ever seen. It was lying with its head turned away from him, washing its whiskers. It was tawny in colour, and had a strange tail with a black tuft on the end.

Then it lifted its head, looked round at Ludo, and yawned, showing all its excellent teeth. It had yellow eyes, and round furry ears, and a mane. It was a lion.

It was *the* Lion. Only then did Ludo remember the paper Gula had given him, with all the signs of the Houses in order. He had been living in such dread of the Crab – and had in fact hardly expected ever to get past it – that he had quite forgotten what lay beyond.

Here were the Lion and the Lady, sitting together by their common boundary; and Ludo was going to have to deal with them both at the same time.

Renti saw the Lion at the same moment as Ludo did, and showed signs of wanting to bolt straight back into the cover of the forest. Which would mean, thought Ludo, that they would only have this boundary to reach and cross again. Their best chance was to get quickly past the Lion before it woke up fully, and into the Lady's territory. Somehow Ludo couldn't believe that an old peasant-woman could be dangerous. Not as much as a lion, anyway.

So he slipped quickly off Renti's back, seized the halter, and urged the horse forward. The Lion watched, interested; then it got gracefully to its feet and stretched, once again showing all those teeth. Renti gave a snort of fright and scurried past the well, dragging Ludo with him. Ludo touched his forehead in greeting as he passed, and said breathlessly:

'Madam, sir – good day to you. If I may … if you'll allow me … In a bit of a hurry, you see …'

'Are you in too much of a hurry,' asked the old Lady, 'to draw some water for me from the well?'

Now Ludo, who was well past the boundary when she spoke, would have liked nothing better than to jump up on Renti's back once more, and gallop on through the Lady's House. There were only two more on Gula's paper, and soon, he was sure, they would catch up with the sun. Indeed the wheel-marks on the grassy track were deep and recent, so recent, that the trodden flowers were just beginning to spring straight again.

But as we know, Ludo was a kind sort of boy, and he knew that certain tasks, like lifting heavy buckets, which were nothing to a boy, were very hard for old ladies; so he stopped, holding Renti's halter tightly, and looked back. He saw that there was a bucket standing by the parapet of the well, with a rope attached to the handle. It stood about half-way between the Lady and the Lion.

He made his way slowly back to the well, dragging Renti, who was behaving not like an old horse at all, but like a spirited young charger who did not in the least want to go back within reach of a large lion. Neither did Ludo. The Lion hadn't moved to catch him, but then perhaps it couldn't go outside its own boundaries; which was small comfort, since the bucket stood right on the boundary, well within the Lion's reach.

He stopped. The old woman was watching him from under her hood. She looked rather stupid.

'Do you think – will the Lion hurt me?' asked Ludo in a whisper.

'I have no idea,' said the old woman, 'but I do know that I have been sitting here for a very long time on this hot morning, waiting for someone to come by and draw me some water to drink.'

'Very well, ma'am,' said Ludo, 'if I can find some-where to tie my horse. He's afraid.'

'I will hold him,' she said, and put out a yellow claw. Ludo would have protested that she was not strong enough – for Renti had been rearing and kicking like one of the King's own stallions – but she grasped the halter before he could speak. To Ludo's surprise the horse immediately quietened down and stood still, with head lowered and ears slack. The old woman nodded at him.

'Now, there's the bucket. You've drawn water from a well before?'

Ludo remembered his mother and his grand-mother, and the old woman who lived at the foot of the stream below the wood at home, and the hundreds of times he had toiled out in all weathers to draw water and fetch firewood for them. And he thought of the Archer and the Bull and of Lykeios, who had seemed so dangerous, but who had not harmed him; and he took a deep breath and walked straight to the boundary and lifted the bucket and lowered it carefully into the well. He drew it up full of clear water, which slopped a little over the edge and ran down in splashes as bright as crystal. He carried the full bucket over to the Lady. The Lion had not moved, except to open his big pink mouth and let his tongue loll out a little. His claws, as big as reaping hooks, flexed slightly, rasping on the stone.

The old woman fumbled inside her skirt pockets and brought out a beaker, which she filled from the bucket and drank to the bottom. Then she thanked Ludo and, though her face was still hidden from him by her hood, he thought she sounded much better than before; less feeble; younger, even.

'Now, would you care for a drink yourself?' she asked him. 'It is very good water, and free to all comers.'

'May I give some to my horse, please, ma'am?' asked Ludo.

'Certainly.'

The bucket was still almost full. Ludo carried it carefully over to Renti, who had stopped watching the Lion and was watching the bucket instead. Ludo set the bucket down for him, and he lowered his head and drank greedily, so greedily that he drained the bucket almost down to the last drop. Then he blew the drops from his nostrils, shook his mane, and lowered his head to the flower-strewn grass near the Lady's feet, and began to graze. He really *did* look younger, and very fit and well. No wonder, thought Ludo a bit enviously, since all he ever thought about was eating and drinking. It was Ludo who had to worry about all the dangers of the journey.

As now. The Lion was still standing on his own side of the boundary, and his tail was motionless, not twitching as it does when a cat (any size of cat) is thinking of springing; but he was still a lion, and though Ludo had never been near a lion before, he knew better than to go within clawing-distance.

'Now,' said the Lady, 'if you are thirsty, by all means draw another pailful.'

Ludo would have liked to decline, but she spoke as if that was out of the question. Besides, he really was very thirsty. So he stood once more on the boundary and lowered the bucket into the well, keeping a wary eye on the big tawny shape which stood so still beside its boundary-stone. The bucket came up, brimming and glittering in the sunshine. Ludo heaved it on to the parapet, and the crystal drops splashed over on the stone and spattered down on the flowers. The Lion watched Ludo with his narrowed golden eyes. His mouth was slightly open, showing all those gleaming teeth, and his tongue was curled, panting, and dribbling a little.

The Lady handed Ludo the beaker. Ludo took it. He found that he, too, was panting a little in the heat. He felt very, very thirsty. He had never wanted anything so much in his life as to fill that beaker and drain it to the very bottom.

But he hesitated, and looked at the Lady. He could see her eyes, very dark and bright, watching him from under the hood.

'Well, boy?' she said sharply.

'Please, ma'am, I wondered – I thought the Lion might be thirsty, too,' said Ludo. 'Would it be all right – would you allow me to offer him a drink as well?'

The Lady regarded him for a moment without speaking. 'The water belongs to all,' she said, 'but you would have to carry the bucket across the boundary. Would you dare do that?'

'If you would let me come back again, please, ma'am,' said Ludo.

'I do not make conditions,' said the Lady sharply. 'Either you go, or you stay. It is your choice.'

Ludo didn't know what to think. On the one hand he was afraid of offending the Lady. But on the other he was sure – looking again at the Lion – that the latter really *was* thirsty. The least one could do for anyone, thought Ludo, was to give them a drink of water.

He set down the beaker, and, walking slowly, as

one should when approaching an animal one is doubtful about, he carried the full bucket across the boundary line, past the stone which said: ♌ and set it down in front of the Lion.

Then he stood very still, and waited for the Lion to drink.

The Lion put his big nose down to the surface of the water, then raised his beautiful, terrifying head again and regarded Ludo. The golden eyes were wide open now.

Ludo licked his own dry lips, and said: 'Would you like a drink?' Then he remembered that this wasn't just any old lion, and added: 'Sir?'

The Lion lowered his head to the water again, and began to lap.

Ludo had somehow never thought of this. The Lion lapped very daintily, just as a kitten laps. The long pink tongue curled round each drop of water, taking it up, apparently, one drop at a time. It seemed a very unsatisfactory way of drinking, though obviously the Lion enjoyed it. His mane brushed the ground, and his tail sank until it was curved just above the grass, and his nose wrinkled and his eyes half closed as the cool sparkling water went, drop by delicate drop, into his mouth.

It took a very, very long time. And poor Ludo, who was dry as dry, had to stand there and listen to the lapping sounds, watching that lovely water going down, and still not getting a single drop himself.

But at last the Lion had had enough. He lifted his head, then sat back with the drops glittering on his beard, and raised a front paw. It was a huge paw. Ludo managed not to flinch, but stood his ground. The Lion licked his paw, washed his mouth carefully, then dried it, and said to Ludo:

'Thank you, boy. I enjoyed that, every drop. I have, I trust, left enough in the bucket for you. Please feel free to finish the rest yourself.'

Then, at the expression on Ludo's face, he smiled. If you have never seen a lion smile, I can't help it; but they can. The trouble is, they don't feel the desire to as a rule. But this Lion smiled, and added:

'Yes, boy, I can speak. Had you forgotten that I am the Lion, and the lord of the House?'

'N – no,' said Ludo, 'but I … I'm sorry, sir, I was so afraid of you that I wasn't thinking about very much at all.'

'I know,' said the Lion gently. 'So I appreciate the water all the more. You are a kind boy, and you are welcome in my House. You came into it in fear, and you passed through it without thought, but now you have paid your way with kindness, and you may go. I shall help you in my turn. Now, take your drink, and then sit down and eat with the Lady.'

Ludo knew quite well what his mother would have said if he had drunk out of the same bucket as Renti, or from the same saucer as the cat; but the Lion was watching him out of those grave golden eyes, and good manners are good manners, so he dipped the beaker in what was left of the water in the bucket, and drank.

I don't suppose you have ever drunk of water like that. We all know that water has no taste, no smell and no colour. But this water had something better than taste or smell or colour; it was like the sparkle of a diamond, like light, like coolness itself, like dew running over wild roses, like rain falling from a spring sky on to young grass. When he had finished it, Ludo felt as if even his skin and eyes had been washed clean and refreshed. The sun shone with a fresher gold, the flowers were cool and bright. Renti glowed as a star-horse should, the Lion's eyes burned like lamps, and the Lady —

Ludo stared. The Lady had thrown back her hood, and she was not old at all; she was young, and more beautiful than anyone Ludo had ever seen. Her hair was gold as corn, and her mouth was the colour of strawberries, and her eyes were blue as the gentians on the hillsides. And more to the point, she was unpacking the basket of food she carried, and laying the contents out on the edge of the well.

Years later, when he was an old man, Ludo used to try and remember everything there was to eat in that feast. Crispy rolls, he said, and roast chicken with stuffing, and patties bursting with meat and herbs and butter, and pastries full of cream and cherries, and fruit of all kinds, from bananas and peaches and pineapples to strawberries and apricots and other things he never even knew the name of. He ceased abruptly to envy Renti, who only had grass to chew, and sat down beside the Lady on the edge of the well.

'Come along, boy. Eat your fill. We have been waiting for you, the Lion and I, ever since we saw the star-arrow fly across the forest. And now I see why the Archer let you in, and why the Far-Shooter himself helped you on your way in the wake of the sun. You are very close now. Because of what you have done, your horse will find his place; have no doubt of that. And you …' She paused, and gave him a kind look, then her eyes met those of the Lion.

'We will both go with you,' said the Lion, 'and see you safely to the forge.'

'Forge?' asked Ludo. Somehow that seemed a very ordinary thing to find in this strange country.

'Yes,' said the Lion. 'If your horse is to stay with the sun he must be shod. Do you think that the hoofs which so far have trodden nothing but the earth can gallop safely up into the sun-tracks of the sky? Look.'

Ludo followed the Lion's lifted gaze, and saw once again, breaking from the horizon ahead into the clear brilliance of the sky, the golden chariot of the sun.

And this time there was no doubt about it; it was closer, so close that Ludo could see the golden flanks of the four horses and their pale-gold manes streaming in the air, and the flash and glitter of the bits and bridles, and the great chariot-wheels spinning on their burning axle-tree. The horses were galloping, straining high and higher up the steep spaces of the sky, with sparks pouring back from their galloping hoofs, and brightness growing round them and falling over the summer world as the chariot rose into heaven. There was Someone in the chariot. But when Ludo looked to see Him he had to blink and look away, and when he looked back at the sky the chariot was gone into the great world of light we call the sun.

He looked back at the Lion, who was watching him with gentle eyes.

'Old Renti? One of those?' he whispered, awed.

The Lion smiled again. 'Why not, child? You have said yourself that he is a star-horse, and if the smith will shoe him, and the Scales weigh him aright, why should he not be fit, after such a journey, for the very chariot of the sun? Do you think it's chance that sent you here with him, to bring him safely all this way? There is no such thing as chance, Ludo. There is a need for Renti in the fields of the sun, so you brought him this far, and now I and the Lady will see you on the last stage of your journey. Lead him now.

No one will ever ride him again.'

Ludo obediently took the halter-rope, and followed the Lion and the Lady downhill across the summer fields.

CHAPTER FIFTEEN

The Scales

The forge was situated beside a river, and the track they followed led down into the water, and vanished in a shallow ford. Beyond the river rose a thick forest of pines, the same sort of forest as Ludo knew at home. This sloped steeply up towards tree-covered hills, with, beyond them, high peaks like the mountains of home. They looked familiar, even to the snow on their summits. Even down here by the forge the air was cooler than it had been beside the well, and there was thick dew on the spiders' webs all along the grasses that edged the way.

But inside the forge it was warm, very warm. The smith, a swarthy old man with shoulders like the Bull's and a lame leg, was heating a shoe in a furnace that blazed like the inside of a volcano. It was very like the smithy that Ludo knew in the village at home; there was the big open fire with its bed of blazing charcoal and the huge leather bellows with the long bar to blow it by. There was the same bucket of water to cool the iron, and the wooden box crammed higgledy-piggledy with nails of all lengths and sizes. Horseshoes hung on the walls; all sorts, from carthorses' to those for the tiniest pony imaginable, and against the wall beyond the bellows bar was a stack of iron bolts and plough-shares.

But one thing here was not like the smithy at home. There was a shelf under the single small window which looked out over the river, and on this shelf Ludo saw the most beautiful little wood-carvings and statues that he had ever seen or even imagined. There were gnomes and dwarfs made of pine-wood, such as his father made, but even more lively and varied. There were deer and chamois and fawns carved from cedar and beech; there were statues made of metal, more delicate still, of fauns and water-creatures and children. And there was a model of a chariot and four horses in a shining metal that looked like – but surely could not have been –

gold. The horses' skins shone and rippled in the fire-light, and the chariot was worked all over so finely that it looked like damask silk. There was no one in the chariot.

But Ludo didn't have a chance to look closely. The smith turned back from the furnace with the shoe glowing red-hot in the long-handled pincers and saw them standing there in the smithy doorway. He did not give them any greeting; neither the Lion nor the Lady seemed to expect it. They did not come in, but stood waiting, one to either side of the doorway. The smith fixed his eyes on Renti, then glowered at Ludo from under his black brows.

'Well, boy,' he said harshly, 'bring him in. Haven't got all day. These shoes are hard to fit, and they can't wait long. Be dark soon. Fetch him in. No need to tie him up; he'll stand.' And soon Renti was standing as quiet as a mouse while the smith lifted his hoofs one after the other and pared them ready for the new shoes. Ludo would have offered to help with the bellows, for he had often done this for the smith at home, but when he looked that way he saw two boys whom he hadn't noticed before, sitting there in the shadows waiting to blow the furnace to a blaze. So he went quietly across to the shelf where the carvings and models were, and stood looking at them while the work went on.

Cling clang, cling clang. The long hiss of cooling metal as the shoe was plunged in the bucket. The wheeze and puff of the bellows and the roar of the fire in the vast chimney. The louder *hissss* as the smoking shoe was fitted to Renti's hoof. The smell of burning hoof which Renti himself, surprisingly, never even seemed to notice. Then the sound of rasp and hammer, and *cling clang,* it started all over again.

It took a long time, and the shadows lengthened outside, but Ludo never noticed the time. Nor did he notice when the Lion and the Lady, very quietly, went away. The little carvings were so beautiful. He examined every line, every tool-mark, and with his whole soul longed that some day, somehow, he might be able to carve even half as well. He, Ludo. Clumsy Ludo, who had never done anything well in his life except look after the beasts for his father, and help his mother about the cottage. Never, never would he be able to do such work! Never even see such things again after he had left this strange, beautiful, and rather terrible country …

A brown horny hand came over his shoulder, making him jump. The smith picked up a horse carved from elm wood, and put it into Ludo's hand.

'Go on, now, get a hold of it, do. Get the feel of it. Rub your thumb over the wood, so. Like that.'

The big spatulate thumb stroked the wood as if it loved it. The horny fingers curved gently round the delicate carved limbs. It did not seem possible that those hard hands had fashioned the lovely little carving. Ludo stroked the wood, and as he did so the smith's great hand closed right over his own, pressing it tightly on the carving, so tightly that it hurt. Then he let go. Ludo's hand was sore and cramped, and when he looked at the palm he saw, pressed into the flesh, the reddened shape of the little horse.

The smith took the carving from him and put it back on the shelf.

'Did that hurt?' he asked, with a smile that was not altogether a kind one.

Ludo nodded, chafing his hands together.

'Then you'll remember it,' said the smith, 'and if ever you get home and pick up a piece of wood to carve, you'll feel the shape in it, the shape it wants to be.' He fixed Ludo with those alarming black eyes, half hidden under the beetly brows. 'Remember that, boy. Everything has a soul. Even the dead wood you pick up off the forest floor has a shape inside it somewhere, and you can carve the outside away like peeling a nut, and find the soul of the wood and the shape it wants to be. You'll cut your hands, and your arms will ache, but you must go on until you find the soul of the wood. And don't think it ought to be easy. Nothing ever is, if it's worth while. But if you want to do it, and if it's in you, then you'll not care how it hurts, but you'll get it done … Now get on the Scales, then you'd best be on your way. The Scorpion's not one to be kept waiting.'

'Scales?' asked Ludo in surprise. Then he remembered the sign that came on Gula's paper after the Lady's, and there it was, not a yard away, burned with a hot iron into the jamb of the door: ⌒

Then he saw the Scales themselves. They were very simple ones, and very big; big enough to weigh a horse. A hook was fixed into the roof overhead, and from this hung a lever; this was the beam, and at each end of it were chains holding a large shallow pan. At present the beam slanted sharply downwards, allowing one of the pans to rest right on the floor. Ludo saw with surprise that the pan held nothing but the frayed piece of rope which was Renti's halter. The other pan was empty.

The smith picked the halter up, and the pan of the Scales swung up and settled level.

'Why were you weighing that?' asked Ludo, surprised.

'I wasn't. I was weighing the horse, and the halter against him.'

'Against him?' Ludo echoed. 'Do you mean you weighed that little bit of rope against a *horse*?'

He couldn't quite manage to keep the incredulity out of his voice, but the smith only nodded as he carried the halter across to where Renti was standing, and began to tie it on. 'They're not common scales, you know. They give a deal of information to whoever can read them, and believe me, it's best to heed what they have to say.'

'Y-yes,' said Ludo, eyeing them uncertainly. They were, of course, the Scales themselves, just as the centaur had been the Archer, and the goat, Goat itself. It wasn't possible to be in awe of them as one was, say, of the Lion, but Ludo found himself asking in a lowered voice, almost as if they could hear him: 'What did they say about Renti, then?'

'That he's ready to go, but the halter will do to hold him with you till the time comes.' The smith slanted Ludo a look from under his brows. 'He's been shod, you see. Something's got to hold him down now, and the halter was just the right weight. Exact. Not a scruple between them. Just as it should be.' He slapped Renti on the neck. 'Stand, now, till I've done.' Then he turned back to Ludo. 'Now, what about you? Your turn now. Come along, we haven't much time.'

'Are you – are you going to weigh me, too?' asked Ludo.

'Of course. Why else are you here? If you are to

come to the Scorpion, you must be weighed in the balance first.'

Less and less, thought Ludo, did he like the sound of the Scorpion, but it seemed there was nothing for it now. He approached the Scales gingerly. 'What will you weigh me against?'

'This.' The smith crossed to the shelf by the window and took down the beautiful little gold chariot. He carried it carefully across to the Scales, and placed it in one of the pans, which immediately sank to the ground with a clang.

'In you get, boy,' said the smith, pointing to the other pan. 'It's my guess that this is just right for you. The Scales will show us soon enough.'

Ludo gave a doubtful glance at the frail golden toy. He pictured the Scales, as his weight went into the other pan, lurching sharply down to strike the ground, and perhaps spilling the chariot out on the stone floor. But he did as he was told, and clambered in – the pan was level with his chest – as best he might.

Immediately the pan moved downwards with him, but gently and smoothly, held by the weight of the other, which swung up to balance it. For all the chariot looked so fragile and was so small, Ludo could feel its weight against his own, kilo for kilo, as the Scales swung this way and that, up and down, till finally the two pans settled side by side, with the beam holding level above them.

The smith gave a grunt of satisfaction. 'I thought as much.'

Ludo sat there, still gently swinging, and looked with amazement at the delicate golden object. 'Is that exact, too? Not a – a scruple between us?'

'See for yourself,' said the smith, with a jerk of his thumb at the level beam.

'Gold must be terribly heavy,' ventured Ludo.

'The thing to wonder at,' said the smith, 'is not that the chariot is as heavy as you, but that you can match the chariot. Now, get out.'

Ludo obeyed him. The smith lifted the golden chariot from the Scales, and carried it back to the shelf. It did not, Ludo thought, seem to be particularly heavy. Certainly not as heavy as an eleven-year-old boy. But he had seen what had happened with his own eyes, and felt it, too.

'How did you know the chariot would be just right for me?'

The smith set the chariot down and turned back from the window. He regarded Ludo with a gleam in his deep-set eyes, as if he was pleased about something.

'I made it,' he said. 'I knew. It is right for anyone like you.'

'*You* made it?' said Ludo, seizing on the one thing he understood. He gazed at the smith with awe, then asked quickly, because he had been wondering about this: 'Why didn't you put a driver in it? I suppose if you had, it would have been too heavy, but still —'

'Boy,' said the smith, and his gruff voice dropped two tones further, coming deep from his chest, 'if you could make an image of that driver, which nobody can, not even I myself, there's no one could be weighed against it, not unless you put the whole world and all the stars as well into that balance, and even then it's my guess that they'd weigh no more than a handful of dust. Now, all's done here. Take your horse and go. He's ready.'

Renti stood by the door. His head was up, and he no longer stood quietly, but fidgeted and danced as if he were hardly able to keep touch with the earth. The new shoes shone and glittered on his dancing hoofs, and Ludo saw that he had been shod, not with iron, but with bright gold.

Ludo drew a deep breath. 'Sir,' he said to the smith, 'sir, how can I pay you? I haven't anything to give you, but if you'll trust me for a day, I'll take Renti where he wants to go, then I'll come back and work for you.'

'Well, and what could you do?'

'I could blow the bellows for you. I help the smith at home.'

'I have boys to do that.'

'I could sharpen your tools for you,' said Ludo. 'I do it for my father.'

'Then do it for yourself,' said the smith, 'in my name. The name itself is too long for you to remember, but I am called the Master Craftsman. You can remember that.'

'Oh, yes.'

'Then work for me. Why do you think I measured you today against my best work?'

'I don't know, sir,' said Ludo.

'Because,' said the smith, 'it is in you to do such work, if you live as I have told you, and measure yourself always against the best that is in you. There is nothing more that a man can ask of his life. Now go, and if the Scorpion will let you, live it.'

'Yes, sir. Thank you, sir ... Oh, they've gone!' This in dismay, as he saw that the Lion and the Lady were no longer there. Somehow he had counted on their escort towards the dreaded Scorpion, who sounded more terrible every moment.

'They can't go with you,' said the smith. 'What did you expect? No one can go with you to the Scorpion. It's up that way, straight across the river. And hurry. You haven't very long.'

Quite suddenly, though the furnace burned as brightly as before, Ludo found that he was shivering with cold. 'What will the Scorpion do?' he asked.

But the smith had already turned back to his work.

'How do I know?' he said crossly. 'He might kill you, I suppose. But he cannot do more than that. Off with you now, and find out for yourself.'

CHAPTER SIXTEEN

The Scorpion

They splashed through the ford. Or rather, Ludo splashed. Renti pranced, and as the golden shoes touched the water the steam rose round them like a kettle boiling. Then they climbed the far bank of the river and passed the sign which said: ♏ and they were in the last of the Houses of the star country.

The air was still and cold and grey. The track led steeply up through the quiet grey forest towards the distant mountain peaks. As they went, it began to snow. The flakes lay chill and light, falling thick and ever thicker on Ludo's head and shoulders. He felt tired as well as frightened, and for the first time began to wonder what would happen at the end of the journey, when – if – he caught the sun chariot and Renti left him for his heart's desire. The smith had said he could not go back; but the one thing Ludo did not want to do was to stay for ever in this cold grey country with neither moon nor sun, where nothing moved except the snow, and a shadow like a grey lizard on a stone beside the way.

The lizard stirred and spoke. And when Ludo stopped and looked, he saw it was no lizard, but the Scorpion itself. He would have liked to run away, but he knew he must not. He stood still, and the creature looked at the boy and horse with its strange, pallid eyes, and lifted its tail high, arched over its back, with the deadly sting in the tip. It was as big as a wolf; almost as big as the Lion. The stinging tail was high above Ludo's head.

'So this is the star-horse that wanted to reach the sun,' said the Scorpion, in a voice as dry and grey as the dust of the track.

'Yes, sir, if you please,' said Ludo, in a rather shaky voice. He had no idea how the creature knew about him and Renti, but he no longer felt surprised at anything.

'And you are the boy who left your home to bring him through the Houses of the star country.'

'Yes, sir.'

'I did not think,' said the Scorpion, in that terrible dusty voice, 'that you would have got this far. But I saw the shooting stars, so I have waited. And now that you have come so far, into this last House, what do you want of me?'

Ludo cleared his throat. 'Only, please sir, to let Renti go through to catch the sun's chariot. He's been shod specially, and —' His voice failed him, and he stopped talking and shuffled his feet in the dust.

'And for yourself?' asked the Scorpion. 'Now that you have brought your horse to his last home, what do you want? To go back to your own again?'

Ludo's heart leaped. But he was still too much in awe of the Scorpion to let his eagerness show. 'They all said I couldn't go back. Is it allowed, then, after all?'

'It is not allowed,' said the Scorpion. 'But whether you go back or forward, it is the same. You will reach your home one way or the other. Which way you go will depend on me.'

Ludo licked his lips, trying not to look at the deadly stinging tail so near his head. 'Yes, sir.'

'But,' went on the Scorpion, 'since you came of your own choice, before your time, and to help your friend, I will allow you to choose which way to go. You may choose for him, and for yourself.'

'Th – thank you,' stammered poor Ludo, who did not understand at all. Renti was standing very quietly beside him, the golden shoes hidden in the dust. There was dust on his coat, too, making him grey, like this cold shadowy valley. He did not move, except to blink when the snow drifted against his eyes.

The Scorpion was silent for a while. Then it spoke again, more slowly even than before. Its words fell as coldly and almost as quietly as the snow.

'They will have told you,' it said, 'that I am Death.'

They had told him, of course. Ludo remembered it all now.

Gula had told him, and the Archer. *You will both find your end in the House of the Scorpion.* At first he had taken this only to mean that this was the last House of the star country; though lately he had known from the very sound of the Scorpion that this last House was the most dangerous of all. But Ludo was only eleven years old, and Death to him had only seemed a story and a legend, and something a very long way off. Now it was here, right across the way which was the only way to go. It stood between him and the mountains of home. It stood between Renti and the sun.

Ludo could think of nothing to say. He stood silent, like Renti, and waited.

'The first choice I will give you,' said the Scorpion softly, 'is for your horse. Because you have been brave and faithful, and because you came of your own will to lead him through these hills and valleys to his heart's desire, you may choose for him either of two things. You may take him back to the valley you call home, or you may leave him in this valley here with me.'

Ludo looked round him at the grey trees, the soft muffling dust of the track, the silver sky overhead. Silence pressed down; no water, no bird singing. Nothing moved except the falling snow. Shadows everywhere, and this great Shadow across the way.

He took a firmer hold on Renti's rope. 'Sir, if I leave him here with you, how will he reach the sun?'

'Look up,' said the Scorpion.

Ludo saw it then, beyond the arch of the Scorpion's stinging tail. At first it was just a slackening of the silvery dusk, but then it grew, a light full of all the colours there are; soft gold and rose and scarlet and violet and green, pulsating, flowing and ebbing and flowing again in waves of radiating light which beat outwards from their centre behind the rocks and trees, as if all the glory in the world was waiting there to burst across the sky.

'Choose quickly,' said the soft, dry voice. 'He is watering his horses, and soon he will harness them once more, and they will be gone.'

Ludo could hear it now; the faint musical jingling of the golden harness. He could see the rippling light reflected from the water where the horses drank.

But across the track lay the stinging shadow which meant Death.

He turned to look at Renti. The old horse did not

seem to have noticed the Scorpion at all. He was staring, with head up and ears forward, towards the light and the sounds that came from the rippling sky.

'You mean,' said Ludo to the Scorpion, 'that if Renti is to stay with the horses of the sun he must be stung, and die? But that if I wish, I may take him home, alive, to his own stable? What sort of choice is that?'

'Your choice,' said the Scorpion.

'What else can I do,' cried Ludo, 'but take him home? Oh, Renti, if only you understood! We can go home – home, back to the valley – they won't be angry then because you got out into the snow. We'll go back together —'

He stopped abruptly. Something was happening that he had never seen before. Renti's head drooped, and from his eyes welled two big tears that ran down his long nose and mingled with the melting snowflakes. Renti had understood. And Renti was weeping.

The tears dripped into the dust. The snow fell silently. Away beyond the forest the rippling light grew brighter, and a horse snorted and a bridle rang.

Ludo put his hands up to Renti's head and drew the halter off. Then he flung his arms round the old horse's neck and kissed him on the soft skin between the nostrils. 'Go, then,' he whispered. 'Go with Him. Be young again. I won't make you go back; I don't care what they say to me. Go with Him now. I'll watch for you, every day. Good-bye, Renti.'

He turned back to the Scorpion, but there was no need for him to speak. The Scorpion was already moving.

What happened next was almost too fast to see. The Scorpion's tail dipped down towards Renti, much as a drooping branch dips above a forest path. The stinging tip of it touched the old horse once, between the ears, and withdrew.

Renti reared. Up on his hind legs he went, with the gold-shod hoofs pawing the air. The light from the sky, brilliant now, shone on bright eye and golden coat and the gilded flurry of mane and tail. The snow wisped hissing off neck and flanks like water off white-hot metal. He neighed once, loudly, then with a toss of the flying mane and a thud and thunder of golden hoofs, he was off, galloping up the track towards the mountains, with the dust rolling back in his wake like smoke.

The light grew. The sky brightened, then flashed as if some thing had plunged headlong into a pool of light, sending ripples across the sky.

'Well?' said the soft, dry voice from the stone. 'And for yourself? What shall I do for you?'

Ludo, standing there in the dust with the empty halter trailing from his hand, and the snow falling and settling thick and cold on hands and face, felt suddenly almost too tired and too cold to think. He was certain now that the mountains ahead of him were the hills that surrounded his own valley. He thought he recognised the shape of the Jägersalp, and beyond it, beyond the high passes full of snow, was the village where his aunt lived, and the little church with the organ that Herr Rumpelmayer played on Sundays, and Rudi's house, and the schoolhouse, and his own home where his mother would be sitting by the stove, and his father would be down in the barn below, and Renti's stall would be empty. Had they even missed him, he wondered? Had they cared? A useless boy, good for nothing except to mind the goats ...

'Choose,' said the Scorpion.

Ludo remembered how Renti had stood there, resigned and trusting. Somehow, he knew that he ought to do the same. He clenched his teeth to stop himself shivering, and looked up through the snow at the shadowy lord of the House.

'Sir,' he said humbly, 'whatever you wish.'

And he shut his eyes.

Something, light as a snowflake, touched his brow. Snow still fell, cold on his skin, but this touch was warm. He felt himself falling away from it, but slowly, as one falls in dreams, drifting down with the snow into the soft dust.

The touch was still on his forehead, warm and damp. There was a noise somewhere, confused, with

voices and a horse neighing and the jingle of harness.
He opened his eyes.

CHAPTER SEVENTEEN

Home

'It's all right,' said someone. 'Look, he's coming round.'

'God be thanked,' said Ludo's father, sounding as if he meant it. He added, gruffly, to the dog which was busily trying to lick Ludo's face: 'Get back, will you? You found him, now leave him be.'

Ludo found he was lying softly in snow, at the edge of the crevasse or snow-pit where he and Renti had fallen. The light was pale and sombre; the light perhaps of early morning, just before sun-up. Snow still fell, small snow which came gently, as if the sky were a big silver skep, which had been tipped up to set the bees swarming. Above his head reared the

157

familiar shape of the Jägersalp, and there was a crowd of people round him – his father, who knelt beside him, his uncle Franzl, Herr Rumpelmayer, the school-master, the village baker and the smith and Rudi's father from the mill. The whole village, thought Ludo confusedly; they must all have turned out to look for him. For him, the boy who wasn't clever enough to do anything but watch the goats and run errands and carry wood and water for the old women …

They were all talking. The words eddied to and fro above his head. He was warm now, with his father's arms round him and his uncle Franzl's big coat wrap-ping him round. Bruno the sheepdog crouched beside him with eager eyes and tail beating the snow. The dog's face and nose were thick with caked snow where he must have dug and ferreted to find Renti and Ludo.

'Renti?' asked Ludo faintly.

'Never mind that,' said a voice on his other side. That was Doctor Kainz, all the way from Niederfeld. He must have set out in the dark. 'Don't worry about anything for a bit, my lad,' he said, and his hands moved carefully over Ludo, feeling and prodding. 'You were lucky. Your father must have got home just after you left to look for the horse. Your tracks were still uncovered. Another half hour, maybe, and even Bruno couldn't have found the pair of you. No, nothing wrong with you that a good warm bed won't cure. Here, take a drink of this.'

The drink was even more bitter than the beer which Ludo had once tried and had not liked, but it sent a lovely warmth running down inside him. He drank and choked a little, and then drank again as the doctor held the flask to his lips.

'A pity about the horse,' said someone, 'but he'd not have seen another year out, I reckon.'

'It was my own fault.' That was Ludo's father. 'I was the last to fasten the barn door last night. And I knew the horse's rope was old and rotten. The boy's mended it till he could do no more, and made a good job of it, too. Trust him; he always was a good lad; you all know that.'

There were sounds of agreement and approval. Someone else said: 'Looks almost as if the rope had been chewed through. The horse got himself free. Strange thing, that. You'd have thought an old beast like that was too wise to leave the barn when the north wind was blowing.'

'Maybe,' said Ludo's father, 'but when they come to their ends, you never know what they'll do. He may have wanted to finish it. But if he'd finished my lad as well …' He cleared his throat violently. 'Well, let's get him back to his mother. She's been fairly frantic. If you give him any more of that stuff, Doctor, he'll be singing like a canary before we get him home.'

And indeed, the warm and potent drink was

making Ludo feel very strange, warm and swimmy
and half-dreaming again. The light was growing.
There was a strange glitter in the falling snow.
Memories floated like dreams. He could see again,
dimly and hazed with brightness, the strange country
he had been wandering in; he could hear the voices
from it, words he would never forget. The Archer's
half-neighing speech, solemn and slow: 'Because
you have kept faith with your friend, you shall go
through.' The smith's gruff tones: 'You will cut your
hands, and your arms will ache, but if you want to do
it, you will.'

'There are better things than being clever.' That
was Gula, whom he remembered perhaps best of all,
the princely boy who had fed him and talked to him
and then saved him from the alien Fish: 'If you get
back to your own valley it will never be quite the
same again.'

And Ludo, as his father carried him towards the
doctor's horse which stood waiting, knew that this
was true. He knew now that the phrase 'good-for-
nothing' simply is not true; everyone is good for
something, and he, Ludo, would find something
which was his own. Dimly, he knew what it would be.
Dimly, still in a half dream, he could see himself with
wood and tools in hand, carving the living wood to let
its soul show itself. His hand still felt the grip of the
master-craftsman in the smithy; the feel of the wood

had gone right down into his nerves and bones and sinews. He would do it. He could do it now. Some day, he knew, people would travel for miles to buy his carvings; they would display them in their houses; they would commission them for their churches; he would even be commanded to make carvings for one of the King's castles …

Some day. But until then he would just be Ludo, who knew all about the goats and the cattle, and who could be trusted to be faithful in small things.

'I did save Renti,' he said suddenly, as his father lifted him on to the back of the doctor's horse and held him there. 'I did save him. He's well and happy, and he isn't lame any more. He's a real star horse now, he's one of the sun's own team. Look, you can see him yourself.'

For just at that moment a marvellous thing happened; the last of the marvellous things of Ludo's adventure with the star horse. With the snow still falling small and light, the sun came up beyond the peaks in a burst of light. Men looked up, and the snow danced and dazzled in front of their snow-fringed eyes. The melting flakes were rainbow coloured, soft gold and rose and green and violet and indigo, then suddenly with a burst of glory they were white and gold as the sun itself plunged out from behind the Jägersalp. The spokes flashed like Catherine-wheels; the four golden horses galloped up the sky. Ludo saw, quite clearly, where Renti's golden hoofs struck the summit of the Jägersalp and sent the sparks from it like a dazzle of fireshot snow, and the sun-chariot started once more on its journey through the Houses of the star country.

The brightness swam.

'Did you see him?' he whispered. 'Up there, with the sun? There, look ...'

'Of course I saw him,' said his father gruffly, and Uncle Franzl said, 'Yes, yes, we all saw him.' They said it indulgently and comfortingly, as grown-ups do, smiling at one another above his head.

Ludo shut his eyes again and turned his head sleepily against his father's shoulder. They were still smiling at one another. But Ludo didn't care. He knew that it was true.

The Zodiac

The name 'Zodiac' is the title which in the ancient world was given to an imaginary belt or track in the sky, which lies along the path of the sun. All the planets lie within this belt.

In ancient times it was believed that the sun moved round the earth, taking a year to complete his journey. The circular track of the Zodiac along which he passed was divided into twelve sections (much as a clock-face is divided into hours), and each of these twelve sections took about a month for him to travel through. So the sun's journey through the Zodiac marked off a sort of heavenly calendar.

Each of the twelve divisions of this heavenly calendar was called a 'House', and each House was ruled by the constellation (or group of stars) which was thought to lie within it. Many of these constellations were called after animals, and this is why the sun's track was called the Zodiac. The name comes from a Greek word *zodiakos,* which means 'to do with animals'. Each House, too, had its ruling planet or deity; for example, Apollo in the House of the Twins; Neptune in the House of the Fish; Vulcan the smith in the House of the Scales, and the Moon in the House of the Crab.

The beginning of the sun's year was the spring, and on March 21st he entered the first House of the Zodiac, which was the House of the Ram. On April 21st he reached the House of the Bull; and after this, taking about a month in each House, he passed in order through the other Houses. There is an old rhyme which will help you to remember the Houses, and the order in which they come:

The Ram, the Bull, the Heavenly Twins,
And next the Crab the Lion shines,
  The Virgin and the Scales,
The Scorpion, Archer and Sea-Goat,
  The man that bears the Watering-pot,
  The Fish with glittering tails.

Ludo's journey started in November, so of course he entered the Zodiac through the House of the Archer.

Each of these creatures of the Zodiac, whom I have called the Lords of the Houses, had his own sign. It was a map of the 'heavenly calendar', showing these signs, which Gula gave to Ludo to guide him on his journey.